Starving Time

Kevin A. Straight

Published by Creative Minority Productions, 2024.

This is a work of fiction. Similarities to real people, places, or events are entirely coincidental.

STARVING TIME

First edition. August 8, 2024.

Copyright © 2024 Kevin A. Straight.

ISBN: 979-8227350176

Written by Kevin A. Straight.

Part 1 - Morning Glory
Chapter 1

THE INCOMING TRAFFIC alarm went silent as the message beacon appeared within the safety-roped confines of the Gate landing. Jim Harris watched the crawl of status messages on his monitor as it connected to his computers, uploaded its mail, and received the outgoing messages in return. He began scanning the message headers as the outgoing lights began to flash, signaling the beginning of the five minute countdown before the beacon once again winked out of existence and reappeared, instantaneously, in a warehouse on Terra.

"Hey Mary, what the heck is 'Security Status Three'?" Jim asked his coworker, as she stepped into the booth.

"Haven't you ever read the handbook? It's one worse than four, which is 'normal'. It means we should be on guard for threats coming through the grid. Terrorism, epidemic, or what have you. Let me see that." She looked over his shoulder at the daily bulletin. One of the best things about working in the booth was being the first people in the colony to get news from the rest of the galaxy—all the news that Control thought worth sending them, anyway. Today the first line read: *Control to all operators. Warning. Possible threat identified. All stations assume SS3 until further notice.*

There were no further details, which was typical; Control was famous for giving remote operators barely enough information to do their jobs. The storage chip on a message beacon could hold many terabytes of data, yet the operators back on Terra always acted like they were using an old Western Union telegraph and paying by the word. Jim scanned the other clear-text messages, but couldn't find any details. The rest of the day's mail consisted of shipping manifests, letters to colonists from family back home, and the weekly demand to the colony's commissioner to explain why he was so far behind schedule.

"It's probably nothing." said Mary, "Just some worry-wart back at Control trying to keep us on our toes. Go ahead and query for more info in tomorrow's mail drop." Unlike Jim, who had taken this posting when he had emigrated three years earlier, straight out of college, Mary had been working for the Gate Corporation for more than eighteen years. This was the fourth planet on which she had been posted, and she had seen it all. "So what's coming in today?"

"More food, if you can call it that. They just booked in four pallets for 10:00 local time. Then an hour after that we have Amy's new hydroponics pods. I hope they work better than her jury rigs."

These days, most deliveries through the Gate were food. The colony had arrived in plenty of time to plant genetically modified potato starts and barley seed, guaranteed to thrive in the planet's salty soils and harsh climate. The first crop had failed completely, as had the second. Now the agricultural experts at the Colonial Administration argued about whether to try again or to give up and rely on hydroponics and algae tanks. Meanwhile the colonists lived on the food rations that came through the Gate every day at a stupendous cost in energy: dry grain and dehydrated powders that, despite the best efforts of the colony's cooks, never resulted in anything but a tasteless mush.

Jim often wondered how the planet, which bore the unlikely moniker of "Morning Glory" had ever been classified as habitable. True, the robot probe which had first visited the system, railgun accelerated decades earlier from old Terra, had only had a few orbits to make its decision before it spent itself to radio a report back to Control. But surely the survey team who had gated through several years later to investigate should have seen what a dog the place was.

But it didn't work that way. Humanity needed to expand. Even now that some of the older colonies had begun launching their own disposable ballistic probes, years passed between reports of habitable planets. The Gate might be able to move people and equipment instantaneously, but they were reliant on the slower-than light probes for their targeting information. Every habitable planet was explored, and someone could be found to colonize even the harshest environments.

Then again, the place may not have seemed that bad from the survey team's point of view. The equatorial areas were only about as cold as Norway, after all, and some of the mineral reports had been promising. There were even ruins from a previous alien civilization, which argued that *someone* had been able to live there.

Mary and her wife Masami came to Jim and Amy's quarters for dinner again that night. It was the same rice and mush as usual, but it always seemed to go down better with company.

"So Amy, how long before we have some fresh vegetables to go on our rice?" asked Mary as she spooned concentrate goo onto the grain on her plate and began forming the resulting paste into chopstick-sized balls.

"Well, the home-made setup that we cobbled together a couple months ago is already producing a bit. I can't really bring that stuff home, though. We've been giving that food to the crèche." She and Jim had talked about that. With the whole colony living on emergency rations, keeping the only fresh vegetables for themselves would quickly have earned the neighbors' hatred. But no one would complain about feeding the children, even though Jim's and Amy's own daughter was among them. Amy suspected that her assistant, Carmen, had been taking some of the vegetables meant for the crèche and selling them, but she couldn't prove it and hadn't mentioned it to anyone but Jim.

"These new units you received today should really be the ticket," Amy went on, "if I can figure out how to work them, at least. Just because I'm a biologist doesn't make me a hydroponics tech. I'm almost afraid to unpack them until I've studied the manual more."

A sudden steady beeping noise from Mary's belt caused everyone to look at her in surprise. Regulations called for the senior Gate operator to wear a remote unit whenever the booth was unattended, but no one in the room, including Mary herself, had ever heard the alarm go off. Consignments never arrived except at the scheduled times; it was dangerous to gate into a space that might be occupied by workers. Besides, there really wasn't anything urgent enough that it couldn't wait a few hours.

Mary thumbed on the display of her remote, "That's strange, it looks like they sent an unscheduled beacon. Looks like it's having trouble uploading. I'm only getting one message, and it's partially corrupted." She fiddled with the controls for a moment, then passed the device to Jim.

"This has to be some sort of prank, right?" he asked. Most of the message had come through as garbage characters, but one line was mostly legible,

...SS 1 immediately. All Gate ... temporarily suspended. Manually inspect all cargo. Post guards at...

"Control doesn't do pranks. And no one would joke about this. Status 1 is really serious stuff: civil war, alien invasion, something like that."

"I've never seen a message get garbled before," said Jim, "those beacons are simple, but built to be absolutely reliable."

Masami broke in, "I thought that interstellar war was impossible. Are you saying Control is being attacked from space?"

"I didn't say that at all," said Mary, "I just said that if we're really at Status 1, then something serious has to be happening: something that affects more than one planet, otherwise Control would just isolate that world until it blew over. Thank you for a lovely meal. I think Jim and I need to go find an operator's handbook and find out what the hell we're supposed to be doing right now. You ladies might as well stay and finish dinner and get the little one in bed."

"And don't worry," said Jim as after he had kissed Amy on the cheek and turned to follow Mary to the door, "I'm sure it's nothing that will affect us way out here."

They had barely made it to the booth when a blinding flash lit the landing area. As soon as the afterimages stopped dancing in his eyes, Jim looked at the landing. No cargo had come through, but the concrete was now cracked and scorched.

Mary pulled down a fire extinguisher and emptied it on an empty plastic pallet which had been too close and caught fire.

"That doesn't look good." mumbled Jim to himself. "It's like they tried to open the Gate, but no matter came, only energy. Is that even possible?"

"Only if everything at Control had just been turned into energy..." There were plenty of modern weapons that could have done that, or even an antique fusion warhead, but Control had been well defended. "We don't really know anything. But I think we should tell the others. I have a feeling it will be a while before the Gate opens again."

The colony's department heads were only mildly surprised to find Jim knocking at their doors just after dinner time. People coming looking for them at odd times was part of the job they had signed on for—even if, most of the time, the "emergency" consisted of an equipment break-down, an underling locking their keys in the shop, or something of similar importance. All of their houses were on the same block as Jim's and Mary's. It had been the first housing block built, and all of them, because of their jobs, had been in the first group through the Gate.

"You're getting all of us out?" asked Yulia Kovalenko of Mechanical, when she saw that Teddy Brigham of Agriculture was already standing in the gravel street, and Jim was in the act of knocking on the door of Lia Djang, the colony's only MD.

"What's going on out here?" asked Julian Reid of Engineering, who had already heard them and stepped out of his house without Jim needing to knock.

"Please," said Mary, reappearing with the colonial commissioner in tow, "everyone just hold your questions until we get over to the depot."

"Dr. Djang isn't home," Jim told her, "she might be down at the clinic."

"Okay, get Amy, then go look for her."

Jim stood out of the way, over near the door to the booth, and watched the others watch Colonial Commissioner Brasini as he tried to take in Mary's explanation. The smoke from Yulia's unfiltered Prima cigarette curled towards the rafters of the depot. No one knew how she got them; the Colonial Administration didn't pay to ship tobacco products, and the brand was becoming hard to find, even on Terra. While Jim had never been to a meeting with this many of the colony's leaders, Mary had told him stories about how Julian always "pitched a fit," as she called it, whenever the Crimean lit a cigarette. This time, no one seemed to notice.

Finally, the commissioner spoke, "How much food do we have here? In weeks, I mean."

Teddy answered the question—his Ag department was nominally in charge of storing and distributing food, "I don't know for sure. It depends on how much each family has at home. You know how it is, people just come in and get what they need, and I order more from

Control when the bins get low. I'm guessing a month or so, though, at the current rate."

"What if we ration it?" Brasini looked profoundly unhappy. Tall, distinguished looking, and friendly, he was popular in the colony. But even his best friends considered him to be more of a bean counter than a leader.

"If we go on half rations it lasts twice as long. Is that what you mean?" Teddy came from a long line of Great Plains wheat farmers. His boss might be on the verge of panic, but Teddy wasn't going to get worked up over a minor matter of impending starvation and death.

"Yes, I mean no. I mean, what's the minimum ration? Dr. Djang, how much do they actually need?"

Djang, who had indeed been at the clinic—doing paperwork, thankfully, not responding to an emergency—pursed her lips. Like Amy, she was in her early thirties. Also like Amy, she had originally been attracted to the Colonial Administration's generous student loan repayment program. "Twelve-hundred calories per day for women and eighteen-hundred for men are usually considered the minimum. At that ration we'll lose weight but we won't die. That's probably around half what our people are eating now." She paused, then went on, "You could probably cut it even further for a little while. Maybe as low as eight-hundred and twelve-hundred. Understand, though, that people will be showing the symptoms of severe malnutrition fairly soon, and they certainly won't be able to do much physical work. On the bright side, our nutrition paste has a high vitamin concentration, so at least we won't need to worry about scurvy, even at that ration level..." Her voice trailed off.

"We should set up rationing now, I suppose," said Commissioner Brasini, "I should go back to my office; we'll need to call a town meeting tomorrow, and I need to think about my statement. Everyone come by my place at," he glanced at the wall clock, which displayed both Morning Glory and Gate Standard time on side by side displays, "07:00 local."

"If I may make one suggestion, Commissioner," broke in Yulia, flicking the tiny stub of her cigarette away from her, "you should be careful how you announce the rationing. It would be better if the person who brought it up wasn't a CA employee. And better still if the actual implementation of rationing was done by one of the colonists."

Most of the room, including Brasini, looked confused at the suggestion.

"You really think it will get that bad?" asked Amy, one of the few who understood the implied warning.

"It will." said Mary, "people are going to be scared. Scared and hungry. And they'll want someone to blame. The only ones less popular than the Gate Corporation, in the person of Jim and I, are going to be you managers from the CA. Having the colonists be in charge of rationing spreads the blame around and makes it harder to decide who to lynch." Unlike most of the colonists, who had bought shares in the colony in exchange for a future distribution of land and other assets, everyone currently in the room was a paid employee, assigned to the colony because of their specialized skills.

"You actually think they would lynch us?" asked Djang, "I don't believe that. Nothing like that has ever happened in the colonies." She looked worried, though, as did they all. Employees of the Gate Corporation and Colonial Administration, and their dependents, made up less than ten percent of Morning Glory's population.

"It will never get that bad," said the increasingly pale commissioner, "not here on Morning Glory."

Brasini did make the announcement himself, in front of the assembled colonists. Since they had no building large enough to hold everyone they stood in the town square, wearing thick sweaters to ward back the chill of a summer morning on Morning Glory. He had to shout a bit to be heard over the wind. Jim watched his neighbors' reactions. He saw disbelief, concern, and fear, but no outright panic. He hadn't expected to; anyone who had already lasted this long on Morning Glory was made of tough stuff.

The commissioner asked for questions and dozens of people raised their hands. "Bill Norris," said Brasini, and pointed at the man, as they had prearranged. Norris was one of Teddy Brigham's cronies—a colonist, and well liked. He had been briefed in earlier and agreed to act as a plant.

"Commissioner, I think we should elect a committee or board or something to keep track of food and make sure everyone gets the same ration."

"Second," said a female voice from the crowd that might have belonged to Masami.

The motion passed with a large majority. It took another hour to elect five members, to serve for the duration of the crises. Teddy Brighams was elected. He couldn't reasonably decline the nomination, considering his job. Jim doubted that he would have, anyway. Teddy wasn't one to shirk responsibility, and he lacked Yulia's paranoid streak. But the other four were all share-holding colonists.

The new created rationing board retreated into the Ag department's barn-like storage building to figure out what they were supposed to be doing, and didn't reappear until midafternoon, having created a four and a half page document, the gist of which was that the colonists had until midnight to surrender all of their "foodstuffs and other edible substances." It took even longer to recruit assistants to go around to notify everyone personally, in case they somehow hadn't read the email. Nonetheless, a queue of colonists carrying partial rice sacks and nutrient paste cartons was to be seen leading out from the front door of the Ag building and past the Gate depot.

"Not carrying much food, are they?" observed Mary. Although none of the colony's 200-odd houses was very far from Ag, most families grabbed a week or two worth of food at a time. Most of the people in the queue were carrying enough for a few days, at most.

"They could be taking multiple trips..."

"Hah," grunted Mary, "or they might have used all those hours of warning they had to hide the rest. I guess it won't make much difference in the end."

"Should we go get our own food and get in line? Amy will be busy down at the lab for a while, so I need to pick up Linda and clear out our pantry." The vegetables ripening in Amy's first, improvised, hydroponics beds fell under the board's order. Probably plenty of other things around the bio department, as well. Since none of it could be moved, the board would need to inventory it in place, so Jim's wife was in for a late night.

"Sure. It's nearly quitting time anyway, and it's not like we have any work to do here anymore."

"Do you actually think this will work?" Jim asked Yulia, closing a toolbox and sitting down on it. He had spent the morning behind the Mechanical shop with some other volunteers helping Yulia cut sections of metal tubing and cable, while two of her regular techs welded them into sections that Jim could lift with the depot's forklift. If all went according to plan (the plan, in this case, having been drawn by Yulia) the sections would bolt nicely into a dish antenna twelve meters in diameter.

"*Blyat*!" she hissed. Jim knew she could speak flawless English, but since the incident her accent had thickened and she had taken to dropping Russian words into conversations. "Hell no! You think I know anything about antennae design, or that we'll be alive in a few years when the signal gets anywhere?" Belatedly, she looked around to see if anyone had heard.

"Then why are we doing it?"

"Because we have to do something. You think we should just roll over and die? Besides, it keeps all you *neschastniy duraki* busy and out of trouble." And that was a worthy goal. In the three weeks since the Gate failed the colony had seen instances of assault, domestic violence, and even vandalism—crimes previously unheard of in a town where a hundred percent of the adult population had passed extensive psych evaluations and background checks. But people were scared and stressed and the failure of the Gate meant that many of the projects which would normally occupy them had been stopped for lack of materials.

Yulia took a Prima packet out of the sleeve pocket of her coveralls. The red and white box now held only a plastic rod, about the same size as a cigarette. She put the rod in her mouth and chewed the end meditatively. She removed it and held it in two fingers, the ends were already looking quite mangled. "Who knows," she said, "maybe aliens will get the signal and come to the rescue? I hope to God they have cigarettes. Tell your wife to grow some tobacco in that lab of hers!"

The existence of intelligent aliens was confirmed by ruins like those a few miles up the road from the colony. Evidence had also been found on other worlds. All of it was thousands, or even tens of thousands, of years old, and displayed a fairly low level of technology. The original inhabitants of Morning Glory, for example, had been pretty good at stacking the local stones to make fences and buildings, and they had had pottery and stone tools. But there was no indication that they had ever gotten as far as metalworking or writing, much less space travel.

The general consensus was that while sentient life was fairly common, it rarely survived long enough to create a technological civilization, capable of inventing and operating something like the Gate. The odds of two such species existing at the same time in the same part of the galaxy were infinitesimal. "Here's hoping," he said, "let's get back to work and get this thing built."

"You got some," said Jim pointing at two gophers hanging from Masami's belt.

"Two," replied Masami, "you should have seen how many I missed."

"I really think crossbows are the way to go," said Mary, flourishing the weapon she carried, "Masami is a better shot than me though."

"No really," said Masami, "these were just lucky shots. The gophers heard the bolts coming but they got confused and ran into them instead of away."

"We need more power," said Mary, "The bolts move too slowly and you have to shoot way up for long shots, so it's hard to aim." She mimed a tall ballistic parabola.

"Can't you just put on a stronger bow or whatever that part is called?" asked Jim.

"If we had one," said Mary, "You'd be surprised how hard it is to find a big long chunk of spring steel around here. Yulia and her people have been working on heat-treating metal, but to get it to work you really need the right alloy. She also has drawings of something using levers and cams and such, instead of one long bow. I don't think she has it working yet, though."

The little mammal-analogs that the colonists called "hairy gophers" lived in colonies similar to those of Terran prairie dogs. They were ubiquitous around the colony, and everywhere else on the prairie. Unfortunately, they ducked underground whenever a human approached closer than 200-meters or so. They were also wizards at detecting traps and snares. Attempts to get to them by digging revealed that the warrens were surprisingly deep and vast, and that it was impossible to find and plug all the exits before the hairy gophers evacuated.

"I just don't understand why they're so good at avoiding large predators on the planet where we haven't found any large predators," said Masami.

Attempts to hunt gophers with slingshots, blowguns, and throwing knives had proved laughably ineffective. No one had yet managed to create a working firearm of any kind, so bows and crossbows were Morning Glory's current state-of-the-art. As Mary and Masami had pointed out, though, finding appropriate materials to make them and learning—through trial and error—how to use them were challenging.

"There are a lot of weird things about this planet," said Jim, to which both women nodded. "Don't worry, I'm sure there's just a trick, and when we figure it out we'll have all the meat we could want."

"I seriously doubt it," Jim heard Masami say, a few places ahead of him in line. They were waiting for their households' daily food rations.

"Oh yeah, and what makes you so sure?" said a stout redheaded woman, one place ahead of Masami in line. "That sort of black market behavior is habitual for people like her. Where'd she get all those cigarettes, huh? Smuggled them and hid them, that's where. Anyway, you know how Russians are."

"No," said Masami, I don't know how Russians are. I know how gossipy busybodies are, who pass rumors about things they know nothing about and make trouble." She stared the other woman down, hands on hips. Masami was one and a half meters tall and slender, but the redhead took two steps back.

Careful Masami, thought Jim, *now she'll go make up stories about you and Mary*. He decided that once he picked up his ration he should find Yulia and warn her.

Things suddenly fell apart. The sounds of a shouting crowd caused people to drop out of line, running to see what was happening. Jim followed them, when he saw that the people dispensing food were closing up shop themselves, to go check out the commotion.

Jim realized that most of the noise was coming from block one, where the colony's leaders had their quarters. "Amy," he breathed, and broke into a dead run. She was most likely still at the lab, but he needed to be sure. The shouting sounded angry and he didn't like the looks on the faces of the colonists he passed.

Reaching his own street, he saw that the crowd was centered on the front door of Yulia's house. *Dammit Yulia, please don't have any hidden food!* Having arrived late, Jim couldn't see much of anything, but he clearly heard a man and a woman screaming at each other. He would have recognized Yulia's voice even without all the Russian expletives. Suddenly, there was a sharp intake of breath from the people closest to the argument. Then a rattle, like someone hacking up a piece of food, but repeating even as it declined in volume. A death rattle, caused by—as he later found out—Yulia's favorite knife having made holes in three of Frank Salazar's internal organs. That would have been bad enough but, unfortunately, Frank had been a member of the ration board. He had received multiple complaints about Yulia and taken it on himself to search her house for contraband. At least, that's what he had planned to do, but he had arrived to find her home, and completely unwilling to let him in.

Frank had been an abrasive sort of person, albeit respected as a hard worker. Things had escalated, and now he was dead. Just like that.

Lynching by hanging is more difficult on a planet without trees, but the colonists were resourceful. They were in the process of organizing a stoning when someone remembered that the Ag warehouse had a high ceiling, and plenty of rope.

Afterward, as Jim stood watching what was left of Yulia Kovalenko sway beneath the rafters of the Ag warehouse he wondered—as he would continue to wonder for the rest of his life—if he should have done something. If there was anything he could have done. Maybe if someone had been able to stop the killings early enough, they wouldn't have continued.

The rest of the rationing board searched Yulia's house later. They found three empty, flattened cigarette cartons, but no food.

The morning after the murder and lynching, Commissioner Brasini called another all-colony meeting to elect a new board member and discuss the incident.

Someone was bound to suggest it, and several did, yet afterward no one seemed to remember who those people had been. Maybe everyone had already assumed that it would come to cannibalism. At any rate, they were starving, and Frank and Yulia were fresh meat. Though he had tried to avoid thinking about it, Jim had assumed that when the time came to eat each other they would draw lots or ask for volunteers—something orderly and dignified. Instead, the first human meat came from a murder and a lynching, and that set the tone for events thereafter.

As is the case with most meat eating species it takes very little to push humans into cannibalism. This can be judged by the strength of the anticannibalism taboo in most societies. Taboos only exist to prevent things people might otherwise actually do. No society, for example, has a taboo against setting fire to one's own eyebrows. But most, at some point, develop a strong taboo against cannibalism. Prior to that point, eating one's fellow humans is an almost universal practice. Everyone has cannibal ancestors, sometimes not very far back. This explains why, once the taboo was set aside and the first two bodies were carved and parceled to households, the colonists adapted smoothly and rapidly to their new diet.

Of course the meat from Yulia and Frank didn't go far among the hundreds of remaining colonists. Meat was back on the menu a week later, though, when commissioner Brasini was found in his home with a slit wrist. The rationing board—now the sole authority on Morning Glory—pronounced it a suicide and sent the body to the Ag building for processing by Teddy Bingham and his assistants, now become the colony's reluctant butchers—having learned to process meat as part of CA's Ag training program.

Various people, including Amy, pointed out that it was curious that Brasini, who had been left-handed, had cut his left wrist. But even had the rationing board had the means or inclination to investigate a murder, most of the evidence was already floating in the colonists' soup pots in tiny chunks.

Soon the rationing board, riding the wave of chaos with no hope of controlling it, began imposing the death penalty as punishment for those caught hoarding. The standard of evidence was low enough to allow people to settle old grudges or preemptively protect themselves from those who had grudges against them. Thus the food supply temporarily increased, and the number of mouths eating it decreased, as the colony consumed itself.

"So you actually think the Gate was destroyed, not just malfunctioning?" Amy asked. They were again gathered at Amy's and Jim's house for dinner, such as it was.

"Well," said Mary, "of course we have no way of knowing, but that was a pretty serious fireball that Jim and I saw. If the other side was anything like that, then they were in real trouble. How much do you know about how the Gate works?"

"Almost nothing," admitted Amy.

"Well, I won't try to explain the science, since I don't understand three dimensional quantum physics myself and I'd just end up confusing both of us. The short version is that a Gate translates objects in three dimensional space by folding higher dimensional space. Objects come through instantaneously, so they don't have time to change into anything else. What came through the Gate seemed to be a lot of superheated plasma, hot enough to crack the concrete. That much plasma doesn't heat itself up, so there must have been one hell of a big fire at Control. And not a regular fire either—I'm talking "surface of a star" or "ground zero at a nuke strike" hot. I don't see how any of their equipment could survive that. We're stuck here until they rebuild it, and then they need to find us again."

"What do you mean, find us?"

"Targeting is the hardest part of operating a Gate. Everything in the universe is moving all the time, not just changing displacement in space, but also rotating about several different axes. And that's not even getting into the gravitational curvature of space itself..."

"Let's not, I get the idea."

"Well anyway, Control has some pretty serious computers that do nothing all day but update models of where all the landings are relative to them. Even then, errors creep in over time. That's one reason they send a beacon through every day. Besides picking up the mail, it triangulates its position in relation to the radio targets on the landing to see how far off the mark it is. When it comes back Control uploads that information as an ongoing correction factor. Most days, it's off by a couple millimeters. But the longer they go without a correction, the further off they'll be—and it isn't linear, the error curve gets pretty steep as time goes on. That's all assuming the computers survived. If they have to work from some off-site backup the position might be really old."

"It's not that bad," put in Jim, "they have the same problem whenever they set up a new Gate for the first time. They send a series of beacons through and correct based on the ones they manage to recover. It can take a couple weeks to get it right, though."

"So this might be a silly question," said Masami, "but could we build our own Gate and use it to go back?"

"Potentially, I suppose," said Mary, "but in practical terms, no. Jim and I are Gate operators, not Gate designers. Assuming, though, that we could cobble up a working design out of the pictures in our manuals, I don't think we could possibly build it with the tools and manpower we have; the Gate on Terra needed hundreds of people and heavy equipment. Even if we could, though, we'd still need to power it. Their Gate uses the dedicated output of two good size hydroelectric plants just to charge the main capacitors. And if we figured that out, there's still the targeting problem, and we'd be starting from scratch, without even probe data.

"Honestly, we're totally screwed. My best guess is it will be years before that Gate opens again, and the food will run out long before then."

"The colony as a whole is screwed," said Masami, "but there are enough resources for five people to live almost indefinitely." She seemed surprised at the looks on the faces of the other three, "What, I can't be the only one thinking it."

"Sweetheart, are you suggesting that we murder everyone else in the colony?" asked Mary, "I don't think it's come to that yet."

"They'll do it to us if we wait. How long until one of us gets accused of hoarding and ends up on a plate? But I'm not saying we should kill them. It's a big planet. Why can't we just steal enough resources to get by, then go somewhere else until they're gone?"

"She has a point, Mary," said Amy, "It's cold, and probably unethical, but I don't like the idea of sitting here waiting to die. I especially don't like the thought of sitting here waiting for my daughter to die. If we can do it, I say we should try."

"Sure," said Jim, "the worst they'll do if they catch us is kill us, and everyone's going to die anyway."

"We need to go tonight," Mary told her fellow conspirators. They had gathered in the Gate booth. The walls back in the housing quarters were thin, and the rationing board had spies in the town. "If we wait, someone will notice." Amy and Masami nodded from where they sat on the floor, trying to keep 3-year-old Linda quiet. Jim covertly gave a thumbs-up sign but did not turn from his lookout post at the only door to the structure.

"The new hydroponics pods are still boxed up and ready to travel," reported Amy, "I wish we had had a chance to try them out, but it looks like they'll run off the truck's reactor. I have enough seeds for at least two crops. They don't inventory those as well as the food."

"Good. How about food until the crops are ready?"

"No problem there," answered Masami, "That extra pallet of concentrate that you and Jim hid should feed the five of us with calories to spare. Are you sure they won't miss it?"

"No reason they would. All the manifests from the last day got fried when the Gate died. There's no way for them to know there were four pallets in that last consignment instead of three. Okay, sounds good. Jim and I still have our keys to the truck and the lift. We'll meet here at midnight and load up the truck, then let's get the hell out of here."

The local moon was smaller and duller than Terra's satellite, but it provided enough light as Mary and Jim used the colony's only forklift to load the colony's only truck. Both vehicles had been gated through in pieces and had the same awkward erector-set quality as the ancient moon rovers. Masami and Amy stood guard, holding sharpened farming tools. No one on the planet had ever been issued real weapons; there had never been any reason, since the planet lacked land animals larger than a Terran house cat. As soon as they finished, Jim and Mary hopped onto the canvas bench seat at the front of the vehicle, Linda between them. Amy and Masami swung themselves up onto the bed between pallets. Jim pushed the lever that energized the electric motors in the vehicle's rear wheels. The truck was powered by a tiny but efficient fusion reactor that would run for at least a hundred years, but its top speed was only slightly above a fast walk.

Jim was beginning to believe they would clear the settlement without trouble when a barrage of flashlight beams clicked on, shining in Jim's eyes and illuminating the truck and its cargo.

"See, I told you she was up to something!" Jim recognized the nasal voice of Amy's assistant, Carmen.

"Halt in the name of the rationing board!" someone bellowed. Then someone in the gathered mob realized that the truck might actually contain food. As one they screamed and charged.

Jim kept the drive lever all the way forward and tried to steer with one hand while he flailed at the crowd with a machete-like tool that the colonists used to clear brush. Next to him, Mary hacked two-handed with the sharpened edge of a shovel, smashing it at faces in the mob. Jim saw at least one person go down under the truck's wheels. He heard screams behind him and prayed that his wife was still alive.

And then, as suddenly as the attack had started, it was over. The mob fell back, either to lick their wounds or to eat their own dead.

Mary wedged the still bloody shovel against her seat and climbed awkwardly backwards into the cargo area. Half a minute later she called for him to stop the truck. Her voice quavered in a way he had never heard before. A short time later, she called for him to start again.

They had started on a dirt road that the colonists had built themselves, really just a track scraped from the surface of the prairie. Soon, though, it joined a road of better, if more ancient make. This led them, after a few kilometers, to a ruined alien city. Before the crisis, scientists from Terra had gated in to examine the ruins. They believed them to be less than a millennia old. Their inhabitants were gone and no one knew what had happened to them. Now what was left of their city would provide a temporary hiding place for the truck. Jim carefully pulled up behind a still standing wall of unmortared stone and shut down his machine. Then, unable to restrain himself any more, he gathered up his daughter and rushed to the back of the truck.

Masami was gone. Amy was pale and shivering but had managed, so far, to stay conscious. "We were keeping them off, but someone threw a rock and hit Masami in the head. They dragged her off the truck and I couldn't stop them. I...Mary, I don't think she suffered much. I'm sorry." Amy herself had been grievously injured. Other colonists had tools which could be used as weapons. A swung mattock had cut most of the way through her collar bone and she had other injuries. She had lost a great deal of blood before Mary had stopped the flow with makeshift bandages. "I think I'm going into shock now." she announced, as she sat propped against one of her hydroponics pods, holding her daughter's hand with the arm that still worked.

"We need to build a fire," said Jim. "We can't move her like this."

"Agreed." said Mary, looking more drained than even weeks of near starvation could account for. "But I don't know how long we can stay. We're still less than a day's walk from town."

"They aren't going to walk this far for a while. Not when they have fresh meat to share out." What he didn't say, which was obvious to both of them, was that they wouldn't need to wait long. Even in a modern hospital Amy's injuries would be critical. Out here, with no proper medical supplies or personnel, she wouldn't survive the night.

They made camp and shared out cups of concentrate gruel.

Chapter 2

"I SAW A MAN," SAID Linda suddenly, with all a toddler's assurance.

"It's okay Honey," said Jim, but he pulled himself up, machete held ready. Mary was doing the same. They both saw the man-shape themselves at the same time.

"Who's there?" Mary challenged.

A figure stepped into the light without answering. At first glance, it was a human male. But the firelight played across the not-quite-human planes of his mostly bald skull, beneath a gray complexion that seemed to have a different texture than human skin. He seemed to be considering the question.

"I believe they used to call me Aorhs. I don't remember if that was a name or a title." He paused then continued, "It doesn't matter." His voice was cold and distantly breathy, like wind blowing through a tomb.

Neither Jim nor Mary knew what to say to this, and the stranger seemed content simply to stand there. The silence had stretched to an awkward length, when the now unconscious Amy began to moan by the fire. Jim edged closer to his dying wife.

"That one is dying," stated Aorhs.

Jim wanted to contradict him, to reassure Amy, but he couldn't manage to form the words.

Again, the stranger seemed to consider. "I think I was a healer once. I could heal this one."

"Hell, Jim. Let him try. We've done everything we know how to do."

Jim looked at the strange man. What the hell was he? A surviving alien, apparently. Or, more likely, a stress induced delusion. "Sure," he lowered his blade and pulled his daughter out of the way, "Go for it."

Aorhs knelt over Amy and sniffed her. Then his hands moved with incredible, almost mechanical speed, removing the bandages from her shoulder. Blood welled weakly from her wound. Then Jim knew for sure that he had slipped over into insane hysteria as he watched Aorhs unhinge his jaw like some obscene humanoid parody of a snake to let twenty centimeter fangs fold out. He flicked a long, mobile tongue, flinging out gelid globs of purple ooze to splatter into Amy's open wounds.

Jim and Mary sprang forward, clenching their improvised weapons. Jim was slightly faster and the alien backhanded him casually, knocking him at least four meters across the campsite.

"Wait," ordered the alien. There was such command in his voice that they both found themselves obeying. By the light of the fire they saw the flesh on Amy's shoulder begin to twitch strangely. Then the wound began to knit itself, as if they were watching a time-lapse holo.

"This one will rest for a time. When she awakens, she will need to feed."

"Thank you," said Jim and meant it from the bottom of his soul. "Where did you come from? Are you from this city?"

Aorhs looked around. "Not from here, no. I came from elsewhere. When your people came your transmissions woke me and I began walking." Another pause. "There were others, once. We fed well, but then the food ran out. I do not know where the others went. I have been here. Waiting. Soon it will be time to go elsewhere, but I do not want to go alone."

"Elsewhere?" asked Mary, "Do you mean somewhere else on this world, or a different world?"

"There is no food on this world," said Aorhs, stating the obvious.

"Wait, do you have a Gate?"

"I do not understand these words in the context you are using them. Soon I will go elsewhere. Perhaps this one will survive and accompany me."

It appeared that this was all the talking that the alien was willing to do. Nothing they said could get him to say more. For hours he stood in vigil over Amy, apparently having no need to sit or rest. Mary and Jim watched him, fighting red-eyed exhaustion with hands clenched on their weapons.

Amy woke up just as dawn was streaking the sky. "Jim," she called for her husband. The alien did not interfere as he knelt over her. "Jim, you need to go. You need to take Linda and get far away from this place. You and Mary and Linda go hide somewhere and stick to our plan."

"I can't leave you." Even as he looked at her face, he saw an unnatural rippling beneath her cheeks—as if her jaw and the muscles around it were reconfiguring themselves, perhaps into a shape that could dislocate and provide clearance for fangs.

"You need to. I'm already so hungry. For meat. You won't be safe. When it happens, I'll try to go back towards the colony. Maybe Aorhs will follow me. You need to go..." she trailed off, losing consciousness again. The rippling beneath her skin had passed downward, and had now reached her shoulders.

"She's right Jim," said Mary, "I don't know what's going on, but I think she's just as lost to us as if she had died. We need to get out of here."

Aohrs' bland expression had changed not at all, as if he was completely unconcerned with what the humans might do. Jim let Mary herd him and Linda to the truck and drive away.

The old alien road had descended into a low bowl in the prairie—dead ground that should hide the truck from anyone who didn't get too close.

"That's good, stop the truck," Jim told Mary.

"The hell you say! We're not nearly far enough away yet." But she had already started to slow.

"Dammit. Stop!"

She sighed and brought the truck to a halt. "I guess you're going to go back and get yourself eaten then?"

"Please don't leave, Daddy." Their raised voices had roused Linda from the semi catatonic state she had been in almost since they had left the camp.

"It's okay, Sweetie. I just need to go back and see your Mommy. You stay here with Mary."

"You know you're a crazy idiot, right? There's nothing you can do. We need to keep going."

"Stay in the truck. Give me four hours. If I'm not back or if you see anyone else, step on it and don't stop until you run out of juice."

Mary screamed into her hands in frustration. Linda began crying. Jim got out of the truck and tested the edge of the machete with his thumb. It was still sharp enough to work. Aorhs might be strong, but he was still made of flesh.

"Four hours. I'll be back."

The scene at the site of their previous camp would have made Jim violently ill once, but the past few weeks had strengthened his stomach. Amy and Aorhs were gone, but the morning light revealed two corpses, already cooled enough to be rimed with morning frost. Both had huge chunks ripped from the limbs and abdomen, as if from the jaws of a large and powerful carnivore. There was enough left of one of them for him to recognize a girl named Dawn, one of Carmen's friends. The other one might have been Carmen herself, but he couldn't find the head, so it was hard to be sure. If it was Carmen, she deserved what she had got. If it hadn't been for her interference they could have slipped peacefully away from the colony.

Jim didn't see any obvious trail leading away from the campsite; not that he was a tracker. Amy had said she would head back towards the settlement though and, since she wasn't one of the victims, she must be mobile and probably traveling with the alien. Was this carnage the work of Aorhs, Amy, or both?

At one end of the old wall which sheltered the campsite was a pile of fallen blocks and other rubble. Jim propped his machete against the wall and walked up the pile then scrambled to the top of the wall. He scanned the surrounding ruins and the open country beyond, but couldn't see anyone moving. He wavered mentally for a few minutes, considering walking back towards the settlement to look for his wife. But even if the alien didn't kill him, the colonists certainly would. Resigned, he let himself off the wall to go back to his daughter and best friend.

Just as his feet touched the ground a scraping of rock alerted his keyed-up reflexes and he threw himself sideways. Turning, he saw Carmen, alive and holding a long kitchen knife. Thwarted in her attempt to backstab him, she crouched and circled to get between him and the machete.

"Carmen, this is crazy. We shouldn't be fighting."

"We shouldn't huh? Even though you guys stole the truck and the hydroponics gear and left the rest of us to die? You always were a jackass. You and Amy deserve each other."

Jim feinted towards his weapon. When she lunged to cut him off he changed direction and slammed into her, letting his greater body mass carry them both to the ground. She flailed with the knife, opening a deep and burning scratch on his cheek before he managed to pin her arm to the ground.

"Listen," he said, breathing heavily, "It doesn't have to be like this. You can come with us. We have enough food for another person.

Besides," his voice caught in his throat, "besides, I don't think Amy is with us anymore and we need someone who understands the hydroponics."

"Really? You'll bring me with you? That sounds great." She smiled, but there was something odd about the shape of her mouth. "Except for one thing," She opened her mouth, and kept opening it, the jaw unhinging and fangs pivoting into place. She released her knife and lifted him easily, rolling them so she was on top, "I don't think I eat rice and vegetables anymore."

Amy's hunger had been sated on the girls she had killed when they had attacked her and Aorhs just before dawn. At the time the need for flesh had been overpowering, driving every other thought from her mind. She thought that Carmen had been one of them, but she had been too aroused by her meat-lust to pay much attention to the faces. As dawn came she loped towards the village, glorying in her new strength even as she was tortured by the thought that she had become a monster. The alien paced her easily, saying nothing.

By the time the village came into view she felt she was rational again and under control. She had decided to make peace with the villagers. After all, all of them were cannibals, all monsters in their own way. She would introduce them to Aorhs and tell them that he had a way off the planet. Surely that information would be enough to buy forgiveness for Jim and the others.

But when the colonists ignored Amy's words and pelted her and Aorhs with rocks she had felt the blood-lust rise again and tensed to spring into their midst, tearing them apart as she had the girls in the ruins. The old alien had held her back, dragging her from the colony until her rage faded.

When they found Jim's corpse in the ruins she had been heartbroken, yet a part of her was glad that he had not lived to see what she had become. She didn't dare try looking for Mary and Linda, but had meekly followed the alien.

When they finally stopped to rest, she asked him, "Did your people do it? Did you destroy the Gate and strand us here?"

"What is a Gate?"

"The device which we use to travel between worlds."

"I have never seen one. I have destroyed nothing. I have not seen my people for a very long time."

After weeks of travel, jogging across the plains and stopping only to hunt the long-haired gophers that lived there, they had reached his ship.

"Well," she said, "I guess it's time to go. Did you have a destination in mind?"

"Elsewhere."

"Right. Elsewhere. Ever been to a little place called Terra?"

Chapter 3

MARY LAY ON THE COLD ground under a hand-painted camouflage poncho, silently cursing the pain in joints that were no longer young, and raised her monocular to her eye. It was an awkward device. She had removed it from a surveying instrument several years earlier and tried to protect it with a wrap of tape. As far as she knew, it was the last piece of precision optics on the planet.

The shed in the bowl below her jumped into clarity and she waited. She was sure she had seen motion below, too high off the ground to be the local wildlife. Yes! There! What was almost certainly the sleeve of someone working behind the shed. Carmen had finally slipped up, and eight years of skirmishes might be over in the next few seconds.

Mary positioned her crossbow, made from parts salvaged from the old truck after it had stripped its gears, and spanned it with the cocking windless in the stock before loading the best of her hand-filed aluminum tubing bolts. As soon as Carmen stepped around the corner, she would die. Not even alien monster healing would save her from a bolt in the head from a 160 lb arbalest.

Suddenly, a random wind gust blew the "sleeve" full out, revealing a shirt stuffed and hung in such a way as to create convincing movement. Without thinking Mary rolled to one side as a javelin buried itself in the dirt where she had just been. She jerked herself into a seated position and fired a snap shot at Carmen, who was already in full charge towards her, retractable jaws extended. The bolt passed clear through her upper thigh—not, unfortunately, a serious wound for her, as Mary knew from unfortunate experience.

Carmen let out a howl: rage, not pain. Mary picked up Carmen's own javelin and prepared to fight a—probably hopeless—close combat. But Carmen had apparently had enough and turned back into the brush, her limp lessening as she began to heal. Mary picked up the crossbow and faded into the brush herself, knowing she didn't have time to span another bolt before Carmen found cover. She sensed, though, that she had seen the last of her enemy for a while. For all her physical advantages and animal cunning, Carmen never attacked until she was sure she had the advantage.

Another beautiful day on Morning Glory, the 2,792nd since the Gate had failed.

Linda Harris was stirring a pot of stew when she heard Mary give the password from outside the dugout. She gave the countersign then moved the heavy piece of pipe that barred the door.

Mary stepped in and tossed a strange javelin into a pile of tools and weapons in the corner, "A present from our neighbor. I gave her a crossbow bolt in return, but I'm sure she's already healed."

"Are you okay?" asked Linda.

"Fine. She never got close enough to lay hands on me."

"You should let me help. Two on one is better odds."

"I don't think one eleven-year-old girl is going to be much help against a space monster, but I appreciate the brave offer. Don't worry, I'll get her one of these days, and then we'll have this worthless excuse for a planet all to ourselves." Those of the other colonists who hadn't turned on each other had long since been hunted down by Carmen, and no one had seen Amy or Aorhs since that night all those years ago. The total planetary population seemed to now consist of one middle-age woman, one pre-teen girl, and a monster.

"How was your day?" Mary asked Linda.

"Fine. I checked the levels in the 'ponics racks then I did my school work, even though I still don't see what the point is of studying French when neither of us even speak it."

"I let you choose any modern language you wanted. Language study is good for critical thinking and makes you better at English too. Besides, if we ever get off this rock you'll still need to get into college." Amy and Jim had downloaded an extensive collection of educational computer programs before gating out. Academically, Linda was actually a bit ahead of most kids her age. The collection had contained plenty of classic children's books too. Their current home had been directly inspired by a Laura Engels Wilder book that Mary had read to a much younger Linda. The hidden back exit and the surrounding death traps had been Mary's ideas, though.

"That pump is still going out on the right-hand pod," said Linda, as she served gopher and vegetable stew into bowls, "you can hear it rattling now if you listen."

"Hopefully it will last for a while longer. I know where there's one I can grab, but Carmen knows I was headed that way today, so I want to avoid the area for a while."

"That's okay. If it goes I can make the one from the middle pod do double duty. I wouldn't want to do it for too long, though. Hey, what's that look for?"

"Nothing. It's just your Mom was worried because we didn't have a hydroponics tech. She didn't know she had already birthed one... Sorry. I didn't mean to bring her up."

"That's okay. I don't mind when we talk about how she was before you-know-what happened."

They continued to chat over dinner, but didn't mention Amy again.

Mary struggled to open the door to the shed. The building had been used to store irrigation equipment back when the colonists had still believed they could farm on the planet. Both she and Carmen had looted it in the past. Hopefully Carmen believed that there was no reason for her to return. That would be true, except that a hollow under the shed floor contained one of several caches of food and tools—a contingency plan in case Carmen ever managed to cut them off from the dugout. The shed could be heated and was sturdy enough that even Carmen would take awhile to rip her way in.

The only problem with the caches was that, given the low-tech food preservation methods they had to use, it was necessary to periodically visit each of them to check and replace the supplies.

As usual, she had carefully scouted the area around the shed for tracks. The hair she had attached to the door was also still there, indicating it had not been opened. She swung the door wide open, crossbow ready, and was glad, though not surprised, to see everything just as she had left it.

As she jammed the door shut with a wedge she kept there for the purpose, she wondered what Carmen had been up to recently. There hadn't been any sign of her for weeks, which was unusual since Carmen didn't bother to hide her comings and goings unless she was actually setting up an ambush. So she was either up to something or had temporarily shifted her hunting grounds.

Mary knelt by at the back corner of the shed and slid aside a pile of soggy packing material that hid the door to the cache.

"Surprise!" yelled Carmen, as she burst forth from the—now enlarged—hole, hands reaching for Mary's neck. Reflexively, Mary rolled back, locking her legs around Carmen's body in a Jiu Jitsu move she had learned over thirty years earlier. Warding off Carmen's choke hold, she reposéd in a hand-strike to the nose which might have killed a normal human. Carmen merely bellowed, then extruded her fangs, her lower jaw dislocating itself obscenely to allow them passage.

Mary battered with her fists at the parts of Carmen she could reach, to little discernible effect.

"You thought you were so much smarter than me," said Carmen, "You thought I didn't know about your little stashes. I lived on your own food and water as I lay there waiting for you." She struck forward. Mary managed to twist just enough that the fangs went into her shoulder, not her throat, shattering her clavicle. She hugged Carmen's head to her like a lover as she plunged the dagger that Carmen hadn't seen her draw deeply and repeatedly into the monster's back.

Using her superior strength Carmen broke free and rolled away, crashing into the wall of the shed. Both women staggered to their feet, Carmen wheezing as a punctured lung struggled to knit itself back together, Mary's left arm trailing blood and hanging crippled and useless.

"Looks like it's time to finish this for good," said Mary as they closed once more, within the confines of the small building.

Linda set down the portable computer she had inherited from her father and wiped tears out of her eyes. The book she was reading, *The Island of the Blue Dolphins*, would have been sad enough for anyone who read it but was especially hard hitting for her. It was about a girl who was stuck all alone on an island for years, just like Linda had been.

"They ought to put warning labels on these books," she said aloud, " 'Not appropriate for people stranded alone on a crappy planet.' " She often talked out loud to herself, just to hear a human voice. It had been almost six years since Mary had finally cornered Carmen and they had, as far as Linda could tell when she finally found the bodies, more or less carved each other to bits. As horrific as that image was, she knew Mary had seen it as her last gift to the girl she had raised as her own. But when the loneliness got overpowering she wished she had Mary back, even if it meant having Carmen back as well.

Perhaps that loneliness was the reason she had taken to spending so much time here in the old Gate depot, where she could feel close to

Mary and the father she had never known. It also helped that the office chairs in the operator's booth were fairly comfortable and that the solar cells on the roof still provided enough power for a couple hours of reading at a time.

She sighed deeply and picked the comp back up, intending to find a more cheerful book, then dropped it when she saw a sight she had given up on ever witnessing. There, on the charred surface of the Gate pad was what could only be a message beacon. She watched as an incoming message light lit up on the long-dead panel in front of her. Hands trembling, she keyed the sequence to download the messages to her father's computer, glad that Mary had insisted she read the Gate handbook.

The message header, which would probably have told Mary a great deal, was gibberish to her but the message below it was in clear text:

Control to Morning Glory Operator. Gate link reestablished. Will translate another beacon 6 hours after this one and every 6 hours thereafter. Please advise as to your status and immediate needs.

As she read the message she saw the beacon vanish from her peripheral vision. She was so overcome that it took her three tries to hit the keystroke to reply to the message, then she wasn't sure what to type.

She forced herself to take a deep breath and relax. Any message she sent would take at least six hours to be transmitted, so she had plenty of time. Finally, she typed:

Morning Glory to Control. The colony here has been wiped out. I am the only survivor. Please send a rescue mission. -Linda Harris

At first she had intended to add details, but she could tell about the aliens, the cannibalism and everything else later. The important thing was to get someone to come get her.

The beacon had transmitted its message at 16:24, according to the comp. She spent most of the next six hours pacing and fidgeting, unable to relax or make herself eat the dinner she had brought into town with her. Would the equipment, unmaintained and possibly damaged by the heat from years ago, transmit the message properly? Would the Gate Corporation bother to send a rescue, or just write Morning Glory off? What would Earth be like? She didn't think she could remember it at all. What would a castaway colonial girl do when she got there? Would she even be able to talk to strangers when/if they came?

At 22:23 the incoming alarm, queued by the previous message, blared for thirty seconds. At precisely 22:24 the message beacon reappeared on the pad and more lights blinked on the control panel. Having refreshed her memory of the Operator's Handbook while she waited she scrambled to open the log file and managed to ascertain that her reply had successfully been transmitted.

She settled down to wait another six hours, but about ten minutes later the depot's aged batteries, overtaxed by all this unusual activity, gave out and the lights flickered into darkness. She had to feel her way out of the building by hand and walk home to the dugout for torches. It was just as well; it gave her a chance to pack. Her comp, which contained all of her parents' pictures and files, was already by the Gate. Once at the dugout she took a rucksack off its peg and stuffed it with her best (though still rather threadbare) change of clothes. A multi-tool with pliers, knife, and screwdriver ends, Mary's salvaged monocular, a magnesium fire starter, her tooth and hair brushes, and a necklace Mary had given her for her tenth birthday. Then, pulling on her parka and a pair of gopher-skin mittens against the nighttime chill, she turned to leave. She paused, though, and on impulse picked up and shouldered Mary's arbalest which had been leaning next to the door, deciding that she couldn't bear to leave it. She doubted that anything she was bringing would be useful on a civilized planet like Earth. But she had lived alone in the wild too long not to be prepared. Anyway, that stuff was hers and she didn't want to leave it.

Linda waited, watching the "Gate Standard Time" side of clock on her computer by the flicker of torchlight, until the digits rolled over to 04:24, the next scheduled translation.

The Gate pad in the depot filled with armed and armored troops deployed backs-in in a circle, guns raised. Linda gave a little squeak and stepped back against the wall, trying to look small.

One of the troops told her to freeze and covered her with his weapon while the rest boiled out to secure a perimeter. Finally, as the calls of "Clear!" started sounding, a figure who seemed to be in charge made a hand gesture and the weapon muzzles were lowered. The leader removed her helmet, revealing a woman with a hard jaw and short blond curls.

"Sorry about all the fuss," she said to Linda, "things are pretty rough at some of the lost colonies and some of our people have gotten jumped as they came out of Gates. I hope we didn't scare you."

"Yeah, no big deal, I guess. I figured it was just some Earth custom my foster mother never taught me."

"I'm Lieutenant Hardy," the woman said. "I guess you must be Linda Harris. Looks like you've grown a bit since the picture the Colonial Administration has of you. Are you really the only survivor?"

"Yeah. At least the only one left now. It's sort of a long story…"

Of course she ended up telling her story…and once the sun came up, showing the lieutenant around the old colony: the housing blocks, the work sheds, the places where failed fields had been (not that you could tell any more), her and Mary's dugout. The grand tour ended at Mary's grave—in a different spot than those of the other colonists, but close to where Mary herself had buried Jim.

"Do you mind if I, you know, take a moment to say goodbye?"

"Go ahead," said Hardy, "I need to check on my sergeant anyway." She withdrew to a discrete distance and made a point of becoming absorbed with unplugging the communicator from her helmet and talking to her subordinates for the next few minutes, giving Linda the illusion of privacy.

"Well, Mary, Dad, it looks like I'm about to leave. I know you always believed they would come for us, and now they finally have. I don't know if I'll ever get to come back. Probably not, I guess. It's funny, though: just yesterday afternoon I was saying how much I hated it here and how lonely I was. Now I sort of don't want to go." She paused for a long moment, unsure of what else to say, "Well, I guess this is goodbye. I know that wherever you are, if you're anywhere, you can probably see me no matter what planet I'm on. But just in case you lose track of me, I'm headed to Terra."

Part 2 - Earth
Chapter 4

THE GATE OPENED ON schedule, translating Hardy's squad, and Linda, away and leaving the sad, cold, planet Morning Glory to the hairy gophers who were once again the dominant life forms.

Linda found the actual experience of the Gate anticlimactic after a lifetime of wondering what it would feel like. It didn't feel like anything. One second you were standing on the concrete pad in a familiar warehouse, then instantly you were standing in a bigger and cleaner, yet similar, warehouse. Mary had explained that the actual machinery of the Gate was underground at HQ, a level below the dozen or so warehouses that served it as staging areas. Once, when they were watching an old science fiction show with teleportation on one of the comps, Mary had pointed out that the sparkles of light and corny sound effects were nothing like how a real Gate worked. Nevertheless, it was disappointing that the whole experience was so...ordinary.

Most of the rescue squad dispersed to go off duty, leaving Linda with Lieutenant Hardy and her sergeant, whose name (according to the nameplate on his armored chest) was Li, J. They stopped at an armory near the staging warehouse where Hardy and Li stripped off their armor, revealing grayish-green fatigues, then unloaded their rifles and handed them to another soldier behind a counter.

Hardy checked her communicator, which she had removed from her helmet and slipped into loops on the wrist of her fatigues which had obviously been designed to receive it. "The old man wants to debrief us in forty minutes. If we hurry we can grab breakfast, or lunch, or whatever meal it is. I'll host you guys at the officers club, they're faster than the line at the mess hall."

There were several other officers in the club. Neither they nor the waiter looked twice at Hardy's guests. It seemed that neither ragged colonials nor NCOs were unusual there, as long as they were with an officer.

Linda ordered a hamburger—a food she had read about but never eaten. The meat was much better than gopher and the bread was divine; she and Mary had grown some wheat but, without Terran yeasts, had been limited to making a kind of unleavened flat bread. This hamburger bun, in comparison, was as fluffy as a cloud and cooked much more evenly than she could have managed at home. The vegetables were a disappointment, however. Neither the lettuce nor the tomatoes were as fresh nor as flavorsome as what she was used to growing hydroponically. The exotic sauces made up for much of that, though.

If the burger impressed Linda, the soft drink that came with it was life changing. She had never had caffeine and not eaten cane sugar in fifteen years (and only rarely, then).

"What is this stuff?" she asked? "It's wonderful!"

Sergeant Li picked up her glass and sniffed it. "It seems to be Cherry Coke."

"I've never had anything like it. I've been up all night, and now I'm wide awake." She took back the glass and had another long pull through the straw. Hardy and Li exchanged worried glances. Apparently, getting the survivor high on stimulants hadn't been in their orders.

"So," said Linda, talking fast, "one thing that's been bothering me a little. You guys are great, but why is everything here so military? I never knew the Gate Corporation was run by the Army or whatever. I mean, Dad and Mary weren't soldiers. At least, if they were, Mary never mentioned it."

"First of all," said Hardy, "we're not Army, we're Marines. I know you don't know the difference so I won't be offended." She smiled to take any sting out of the words, "Secondly, the military didn't run things until the incident. Military security at the Gate was one of the requirements the corporation had to agree to if they wanted to start operating again at all."

"What really happened? In the incident, I mean?"

Li glanced at his wrist meaningfully. "We need to go see my boss now," said Hardy, "and I don't want to be late, but I'll give you the short version as we walk.

"Basically, it was an act of terrorism. You know what terrorists are, right? They hit us several places at once, including Gate HQ, where they must have had multiple people on the inside. As far as we can tell they opened a bunch of Gates in quick succession, including one that went straight to the corona of a star. They managed to melt not just the old HQ building, but a couple of Gate depots, and the surrounding blocks of buildings, on colonies. It's lucky Morning Glory only got a little singed. There were a lot of casualties here on Earth, and some people didn't want to use Gates anymore at all afterwards, especially when we still thought the whole thing might be an accident.

"Luckily for the million or so people in the colonies, wiser heads prevailed. But it took a long time to rebuild, and now there are a lot more safeguards. Including us. Especially us. Any new terrorists will have to get past our whole battalion."

They had arrived at the door of the office. Hardy knocked three times, then stepped inside, Li and Linda following closely.

"Sir, here is Ms. Harris from Morning Glory. Linda, this is Colonel Singh." Colonel Singh was a man in his forties with medium brown skin and incisive, intelligent eyes. His shoulders were rounded but powerful looking and the hand he reached out to take Linda's was huge and solid. He wore the same uniform as the rest of his battalion, except for a neatly wrapped black turban. "Nice to meet you, Linda. It sounds like you've had a rough time."

Of course Singh wanted to hear everything that Linda had already told the lieutenant, then get a full report from the lieutenant herself, then ask them both questions about the pictures the other Marines had taken. At one point Sergeant Li had to go and get Linda another Cherry Coke, when the first one began to wear off and lack of sleep made her begin slurring her words.

Finally, the colonel decided he had enough and released them. "Where should I put her for tonight, Lieutenant?" he asked, "I don't want to open up a colonial dorm for one person. I suppose we can find her a spot in the BOQ..."

"I have a spare bedroom, Sir. And my apartment is only about a mile from here."

"Good. Keep her handy in case we need anything else for the report. It looks like Morning Glory is a complete write off, but we need to convince the politicos about that so they don't send us back to make sure. Dismissed. All three of you, please get some rest."

"Sorry 'bout the mess," said the lieutenant, as she keyed in her code and opened the door of her flat. It was one of six on the second floor of a courtyard apartment building, one of several such buildings scattered just outside the Gate complex.

Linda stepped in and looked around. She was in a medium-sized rectangular room with a kitchen at one end and a couch and a cabinet which probably contained entertainment electronics at the other. Three closed doors lead deeper into the flat. She couldn't see any mess at all, unless Hardy was referring to the dirty coffee cup and plate on the kitchen snack bar.

"You're in the room on the far right," Hardy continued, "The sheets should be clean. I'll find a towel for you. Do you want to take the first shower?"

Linda opened the door to her room and found the light switch, which was similar to the ones used in the colony buildings but, unlike those, was still connected to a working light fixture. Her bedroom was a ten-foot-square room with a desk and a single bed, but no other furnishings. Bare nails on the walls showed where a previous occupant had hung pictures or other decorations. "Is this a typical Earth home?" she asked.

"Pretty much. This is a nicer building than some. But size-wise, this unit is pretty typical for two single people. My flatmate finished his hitch two months ago and went home to Reno and I haven't found another yet. That's why I have the extra room."

"This isn't much different from the family housing on Morning Glory. It's just weird to see it clean and lived-in, if you know what I mean. We always lived outside the town and just came into places like this to scavenge."

"Well, speaking of scavenging, feel free to eat anything you find in the fridge. It's usually mostly condiments, but you never know."

The communicator on Hardy's wrist began to pulse and she touched a button to answer it. "This is Hardy," she said, holding it to her ear. Then, "It's for you." She slipped the device out of its attachments and handed it to Linda, who had never used a telephone in her life. Luckily, it turned out to be pretty intuitive.

"Linda Harris?"

"Yes."

"Sorry to bother you, I know you've had a long day. This is Mark Ragasa from the Gate Corporation. I'm a public relations technician."

"Okay."

"I won't bother you much tonight, but I'd like to call you tomorrow and have a chat. Will that be okay?"

"Okay."

"Great. In the meantime, though, there is something I need to request: please don't talk to anyone until you and I have had that chat. Especially, don't talk to reporters. Sometimes they like to badger newly arrived colonials, especially when they have a good story like you. Just ignore them, and don't answer. Can you do that?"

"Sure."

"Good, I'll call you tomorrow."

Mark was true to his word, calling on video just as Linda and the lieutenant were finishing a breakfast of instant oatmeal and black coffee (the former of which seemed mildly convenient, the later utterly disgusting to Linda). Lieutenant Hardy routed the call to the entertainment computer in the living room so she could retain her wrist com.

Mark Ragasa was a slender man in his thirties with old acne scars, a friendly smile, and facial features Linda would later learn to associate with Pacific islanders.

"Hi Linda, how'd you sleep?"

"Like a log. It's not every day I get rescued off a desert planet then spend six hours answering questions."

"Sorry about all the questions. Talking to survivors is the only way we can know what happened with the colonies. It's hard on you, though, because you're the only one from Morning Glory."

"Are there a lot of us? Survivors, I mean."

"Sure. At least half the lost colonies actually gained population while they were out of contact. Just Jackpot and Cornucopia between them have over half a million people. Only a few died out completely. As I understand it your colony had...special circumstances. Most places did better."

"Yeah, you could say that."

"So anyway, here's the situation: there are people here on Earth who think any sort of colonization is a bad idea, and they hold up the Gate disaster as an example of the sort of thing that can go wrong; never mind that it was a one time event that can never happen again because we've increased security so much. These people don't really care about colonists. The whole thing is really about money and politics. But they and their buddies in the media will happily hype up your story about Morning Glory to scare the voters. What I'm asking is that you not talk to them until you know more about the whole situation yourself."

"I can do that."

"And eventually, if you do talk to them—and I hope you will keep me in the loop if that happens—I don't think you should mention 'aliens.'"

"Because I'll scare people?"

"Some, but most will just think you're crazy. Don't take this the wrong way, but you're the only living person who has seen one of these 'aliens,' and it sounded like she was already dead."

"I may not have seen her up close until she was dead, but we played hide-and-seek with her for years. I also saw the other one, when I was little. Trust me, they're very real."

"Okay. The Gate Corporation believes you. But I don't think it's a can of worms you want to open. The main story here isn't aliens—whom we will probably never run into again anyway—it's how a courageous young woman defied the odds and survived, setting an example for the whole colonization program. I plan to tell that story, but I want to make sure you're on board with me. That's the story that will be best for the colonists, the Corporation, and even for those idiot Earth Firsters. You understand?"

"Sure. I won't talk to anyone without checking with you."

"Thanks. I really appreciate it. We actually have a news conference scheduled for tomorrow evening, but all the reporters we invited know the rules and I'll have time to meet with you just before. I'll see you then."

After getting off the phone, Linda followed Lieutenant Hardy (whose first name was Andrea) back to the Gate complex where she was ushered into a conference room full of staff officers. They asked several of the same questions as Hardy and Singh had, but it was clear they were mainly interested in Aorhs...and Carmen.

"You're quite sure she was human until she met the other alien?" asked a captain to whom the others in the room seemed to defer, even though several seemed older and had more ribbons and patches on their uniforms.

"I was only a little girl. But my mother worked with her for years, and never told Mary, who was one of her best friends, that there was anything weird about her."

"And then after she met the other one she got big fangs and super powers..."

"Listen, if you don't believe me just say so."

The captain looked at one of the scientists and gave a short nod. The scientist, a middle aged woman with a gray-streaked bob hairstyle cleared her throat. "We probably wouldn't have believed you, but we have evidence. The platoon leader who extracted you took it on her own authority to exhume the graves you said contained Ms. Ortiz and Ms. Adler and take pictures. Would it bother you if I showed the pictures on the projector?

"Honestly, yes."

"That's fine. Just to summarize, one grave contained skeletal remains of a human female, consistent in height and age range with Mary Adler's records. From what we can tell from the pictures her dental records also match. The other grave contains a humanoid skeleton. It differs from a *homo sapiens* skeleton in several key respects, including having an extra cervical vertebra and significantly different geometry of the skull and mandible. And fangs. So yes, we believe you."

"Did they, you know, re-burry them afterwards?"

The captain spoke. "We did. But we sent a detail this morning to go back and get the remains of Carmen Ortiz, or whatever that was."

"We think it definitely was her," said the scientist, "at least in the beginning. Marine platoons carry kits to collect DNA samples. Apparently they sometimes recover bodies that they can't identify any other way. Anyway, we've been analyzing the samples they took. Based on DNA records the Colonial Administration keeps, one of those bodies is a perfect match for Ms. Adler. The other one, the one with the fangs, is about a 95% match for Ms. Ortiz. That means that genetically it's closer to her than it is to any other living thing of Earth origin, albeit more different than any two Earth animals are from each other. But as far as we can tell large segments of DNA have been completely rewritten in a way that suggests deliberate genetic engineering.

"The question is how. You say the first alien secreted some sort of saliva..."

"Yeah"

"What we don't understand is how, if the virus or whatever it was contained in saliva, the whole planetary population didn't get infected instead of being killed off."

"Mary had a theory about that..."

Seven-year old Linda sat cross-legged on the floor of the tent as Mary pulled items from her latest "goodie bag" (a selection of salvage gleanings bundled up in a spare poncho). She had already removed a surveying unit, from which she hoped to extract a working telescope, and some tools they had been looking for to finish breaking down the truck. Now she took out her *pièce-de-resistance*, two portable computer tablets. "They should have some good new books and movies," her expression darkened briefly, "the house I took them from used to have kids the age you are now."

"Great!" said Linda, "I'm so tired of the old ones! Let's plug them in now and charge them up."

"Go ahead," said Mary, and watched as Linda facilely plugged the tablets into the octopus-like power distribution strip that Mary had jury-rigged onto the truck's reactor.

"Did you see anyone else this trip?" asked Linda.

"See? No, I didn't see them. But I know they're there. Not as many as last time, though—probably only four or five left, forted up in different buildings. It's hard to believe there's any food left in town for them to eat after all these years. I doubt they'll last through the winter, even if Carmen doesn't get them.

Linda nodded. Savage colonists and Carmen were simple facts of her young life, much like Morning Glory's brutal winter storms. "How come there aren't more Carmens?" she asked.

"Isn't one enough?"

"No, I mean, if the monster thing is in Carmen's spit, and she's been going around biting people this whole time, how come there aren't more monsters?"

"I'm not sure. Most of the time if Carmen bites someone she eats them before they can turn into anything. But some of them must have gotten away from time to time...the best I can come up with is that she's like a rattlesnake."

"A what?"

"A kind of poisonous snake that used to be pretty common where I grew up. I don't know if it's true, but I always heard that baby rattlesnakes are more dangerous than full-grown ones, because the babies don't know how to control their venom yet. So a big daddy snake just shoots enough to get the job done, but if a baby bites you it pumps every drop it has. I think Carmen knows how to control the monster juice now, and she doesn't want to make competitors for herself."

"That makes sense. Does that mean my Mom was like a baby rattlesnake when she made Carmen?"

"It's as good a theory as any. We'll but we'll probably never know for sure. I certainly don't plan to get close enough to Carmen to ask her."

They let her go around noon and, since Hardy was still on duty for three more hours, she made her way back to the apartment on her own. Once there she figured out how to watch holo on Hardy's entertainment center. She thought most of the programming was phenomenally stupid, yet fascinating for what it showed her of the culture in which she would now need to live.

One thing she realized quickly was that she would soon need different clothes. Not only were both her outfits too warm for the season, but they were strictly workwear, and had been worn hard. She didn't draw stares around the Gate complex, where people were used to colonials coming and going from other planets, but she could tell from the holo programs that the usual Terran standard of dress was quite a bit fancier. That brought up the larger problem of money: she had none. In the short term she could crash with Hardy and take her meals at the Marine mess hall, but she might need to get a job soon.

She lingered briefly on a quiz show, which reminded her of a louder, competitive version of some of the educational programs she had used when she was six. After that she saw three advertisements. At least she thought they were trying to sell something, but amidst all the music and pictures she couldn't tell what the actual product was. Next was a program of highlights from that week's North American Women's Sumo tournament. She watched this much longer than she meant to, mesmerized by the sheer surreality of it, even though she had no idea what was going on, other than that the object was to knock the other woman over or push them out of the ring. The *rikishi* were huge—bigger than anyone she'd ever seen—and clearly very powerful, but she couldn't help wondering how one of them would do in a real fight against, say, Mary, or Andrea Hardy. Not well, she thought, as long as there was room to maneuver. When Mary had first begun teaching Linda how to fight she had told her, "Forget style. Forget fairness. Especially, forget everything you've seen in those old movies. Even if you never have to fight Carmen, and I sure as hell hope you don't, most people you run into will be bigger or stronger than you. So you win by being sneakier and nastier than them. And always cheat if you can. There's no such thing as a fair fight, especially out here in the colonies, so try to make sure it's unfair in your favor."

Finally she stopped the stream of the sumo program. Scrolling listlessly through the pages of available programs she saw a show called "Mysteries of the Lost Colonies" which was tagged as a documentary. Playing the stream, she was greeted by a scene of cave-man-like characters (three actors doing their best to look like a whole tribe) dancing around a fire and waving clubs.

"Cut off from civilization on a savage frontier", began the narrator, "they were forced to descend into savagery to survive. Now, reconnected with a universe they can't hope to understand, what will become of the *lost colonies*?"

Considering what had happened on Morning Glory, she certainly couldn't quibble with the "descend into savagery" statement. She doubted that many colonists had worn fur loin-cloths. She and Mary, at least, had stuck with the nearly indestructible colonial-issue dungarees.

The program went into an animated sequence about the history of colonization. Some of the visuals were pretty, though Linda would have liked more information about how the railguns and the deep-space probes actually worked. When the story reached the point of the establishment of the first permanent colony the scene cut to an expert, a man with wire-rim glasses and a black beard that was too big for the rest of his body who had apparently written a book on the colonies.

"From the moment the Gates were discovered, they were hyped as a solution to all the problems of the human race. Politicians started talking about our 'expansive destiny' and huge amounts of money and manpower were poured into the Gate infrastructure. But the fact is that the whole colonization program has been an expensive boondoggle from the beginning.

"Unlike the mining stations in the belt, or the Lagrange habitats, planetary colonies produce few products that we don't make on Earth—they keep most of them for their own immediate use. Balance that against all of the expensive tech, not to mention the trained specialists to use it, that needs to be gated out in the other direction.

"At the same time, and contrary to what politicians maintained in the beginning, the Gate program has a negligible, essentially a zero, effect on Earth's population. Even if they shipped people out twenty-four hours a day, which they can't, it wouldn't make a difference.

"So you basically have a program that was hemorrhaging money before the attack, and had to be mostly rebuilt after the attack just to save a few survivors."

That was sobering. Linda wondered how many Terrans agreed with the expert. The show continued with animations supposed to depict the attack and clips of other experts. Much of the information was either repeated or seemed to be outright fluff, designed to fill time. Some of the experts argued for evacuating all of the colonies. Another one proposed, in all seriousness, that some of them be turned into pure penal colonies, thus easing Terra's overcrowded prison problem. Linda kept waiting for a colonial expert to appear, but none did. It seemed the "colonial problem" was something to be debated by Terran intellectuals, who had probably never gated in their lives. Was all coverage of the colonies this slanted? At least she, a *bona fide* lost colony survivor, would get a say later at the press conference.

Linda was back to the compound in plenty of time for the press conference. Not that she could have been late if she had tried, since an apologetic looking Sergeant Li arrived at the flat forty-five minutes beforehand to collect her.

"Remember," Ragasa told her, just before he stepped to the podium to introduce her, "stick to the truth but don't mention any aliens and don't volunteer information." He stepped out of the stage wings and up to the podium,

"Ladies and gentlemen of the press, good evening. It gives me great pleasure tonight to introduce to you a very brave young woman who beat the odds. Linda Harris is the only survivor of the Morning Glory colony and she was rescued yesterday by the efforts of the Terran Marine Corps and the Gate Corporation. Linda?"

Linda stepped to the podium and made the mistake of looking out. There were dozens of reporters on the rows of chairs in the room. Camera operators and hovering drones lined the aisles on the sides and back. It was more people than she had ever seen in one place, at least since she was a child and the whole village had tried to lynch her family. She felt her stomach clench and the edges of her vision began to go dark.

"Uh, hello?" she began. Her voice sounded unnaturally flat through the microphone.

Instantly, every reporter in the room raised their hand. Ragasa pointed at a woman in the front row, "Ms. Clark."

"Linda—can we call you Linda?—How old were you when the Gate incident happened, and how old are you now?"

"I was three. I'm almost eighteen now." Linda realized she was gripping the sides of the podium hard, as if to keep from being thrown off. Mark Ragasa was already giving the go-ahead to the next reporter.

"So you lived all alone for fifteen years?"

"No, I lived with my foster mother for more than half that time. " and Carmen, but she wasn't supposed to mention her, "I was only alone at the end."

The questions continued in the same vein, and she slowly managed to relax. But then the tone began to change. Ragasa looked increasingly flustered as he physically interposed himself between her and the reporters, answering "No comment." on her behalf to several questions in a row.

"Do you blame the Gate Corporation for leaving you stranded?"

"Do you think that it was responsible to settle a marginal world like Morning Glory that couldn't feed itself?"

"Have you had any contact with survivors from the other lost colonies?"

"Is it true that your whole colony descended into cannibalism?"

At last someone asked, "Can you shed any light on the rumors that Morning Glory was attacked by aliens?" causing Colonel Singh to rise from his chair.

"This conference is over!" he stated in command voice, "You so-called media professionals should have more class than to badger a young woman with this ridiculous nonsense." He pointed to the stage door, causing Ragasa to gently pry Linda's fingers from the podium and lead her away.

"How'd that circus happen?" he asked Ragasa, "I thought you said those were the reporters we could trust."

"Sorry Colonel. They were. I don't know what's gotten into them, but it's pretty clear we have a leak."

"You think?"

"We'll find it, and we'll make sure whoever it is has a seriously bad day." he turned to Linda, "Good job out there Linda..." Linda was doubled over. Her tunnel-vision was even worse and she couldn't seem to get enough air, no matter how much she breathed. "Damn, she's having a panic attack. Go call a medic. Linda, listen to me: take deep breaths."

Linda let herself slide down the wall against which she had been leaning until she was sitting on the floor and tried to follow his advice.

Shortly afterwards the medic arrived and, after a quick exam, gave her a shot from a pneumatic hypo that quickly calmed her. Andrea Hardy arrived immediately afterwards to walk her home to the flat. She took no obvious lasting harm from the incident, but hoped Ragasa and Singh would not expect her to hold any more press conferences...at least until she got used to Earth and its crowds.

A day or two later, at breakfast, Linda brought up her money issues with Hardy.

"I'm sure you have some money coming," said the lieutenant thoughtfully, "your parents would have left you something, I think. If nothing else, I'm not above passing the hat in my company to give you some money to get started, but I really doubt it will come to that. I think you actually need to talk to a lawyer. Probably not one of the Gate Corporation's lawyers, though. We have a Navy JAG back at Brigade. I think I can get you an appointment with her even though you're not military, considering the circumstances."

The Navy lawyer had an opening the next Tuesday. "Brigade" turned out to be an office building in a gated military park two towns over which was full of uniformed Marines doing clerical tasks. Singh gave Hardy permission to drive Linda there in a ground car from the motor pool. The Navy lawyer, Lieutenant Wurthers, turned out to be around Hardy's age ("doing a hitch to pay off law school", Hardy had explained in the waiting room).

"First thing's first," she told Linda, "this is for you. It was sitting in an office downstairs, but I rescued it. No telling how long it would have taken to catch up to you, otherwise." She handed Linda an identification card with her name and picture. "Now you're officially a member of the human race.

"Now Andrea tells me you've had some money worries. I can tell you right now that you don't need to worry. Your father was a Gate Corporation employee and they have good survivor benefits. Normally you would split them with your mother but, since she's missing and presumed dead I believe you will probably be able to draw the whole amount.

"Now as far as inheritance goes, your parents were not wealthy. However, since they were officially assigned to Morning Glory they were allowed to buy shares in the colony, and that seems to be where they put what savings they did have—some in their names and some in yours. The way it worked was that all the colonists and specialists were allowed to buy shares up to a certain date. After that date, which passed more than five years ago, by the way, the shares could be converted into land or mineral claims on the planet. Of course the actual rules are pretty complex, but that's the short version.

"Where it gets complicated, is the fact that there was a survivorship clause in the colonial charter. In theory, as the last surviving colonist, you now own all of the rights. If that's the way the court sees it, you will eventually own forty-nine percent of Morning Glory. The Gate Corporation owns the other fifty-one percent, but even forty-nine percent of a whole planet is a lot of land. All of that is likely to be tied up in court for years, though. You're the only sole survivor, but other lost colonies were down to very small populations. The corporation and the government are going to resist giving that big a windfall to a small number of individuals.

"So that's your parents. Did you know that Mary Adler filed a will in your favor about a year before she died? It apparently came over on the first message beacon and, since she doesn't have any other relatives, it's unlikely to be challenged. Anyway, it looks like she followed all the forms and signed it bioinformatically, so it would be valid regardless.

"It turns out that Mary and Masami had a respectably large nest-egg tucked away. Furthermore, it looks like Mary bought colony shares on every planet she ever worked on, and a lot of them have already been converted. As soon as that will clears probate you will own real estate and mineral rights on several different planets, most of them more developed than Morning Glory. Of course taxes are going to take a bite, but in the end you are going to be a rather affluent young woman."

Linda realized her mouth had been hanging open for most of the attorney's speech and willed it to close. "I never knew. Mary never said anything. What do I do now?"

Lieutenant Wurthers grinned, "Well, you should probably start paying Andrea rent. That is, if you plan to stay there and not get a place alone. I would advise staying, actually. You'll have less culture shock if you aren't living alone, and she needs a flatmate anyway. Beyond that, I would advise hiring a good accountant or financial planner. And at some point, you should probably go to college."

"Mary always wanted me to go to college..."

"And for right now, I arranged for the Gate Corporation to cut you a check for your first month's benefit. The paymaster's office downstairs can cash it for you. Andrea can show you where the window is."

Linda took the check. "Anyone want to go out to lunch? I guess I'm buying."

Chapter 5

"SO AS YOU KNOW, WE have an essay test coming up, and I thought we could use a day to get ready," the instructor began, "so just to get the ball rolling, what if I were to ask you to explain the causes of the American Revolution?"

Linda settled herself for a boring forty-five minutes, knowing that she didn't need help getting ready for the test. On the advice of an admissions counselor she had signed up for a term of classes at a junior college near her flat. The theory was that, given her unconventional education, she would have a better chance of getting into a good university if she showed that she could do well in a conventional academic setting. She wondered if the counselor had expected her to freak out and start shooting people with her crossbow if she had to be around normal people. To her relief, if not surprise, junior college was horribly easy. In this history class, for instance, they had spent the past few weeks discussing things she had read about when she was twelve. She had no real worries about her ability to get a report card full of A's and move on to bigger and better things.

Socializing with her fellow students had been a bit tougher—mainly because they seemed to have so little in common, other than school—which most of them seemed to think was actually hard. She just wasn't that into talking about clothing, and she had never heard of most of the games or music that they thought were cool. Conversely, she doubted most of them wanted to talk about hydroponics or gopher hunting or how to avoid a psychotic alien vampire bitch, which were the things she knew the most about. The one thing that made the situation a little better was that several Marines from the Gate complex battalion were currently taking classes at the college, and they not only knew her as the lieutenant's flatmate, but actually were interested in talking about survival skills for out in the colonies—which was understandable, considering what they did for a living. Unfortunately most of them only took one or two evening classes and didn't hang around the college much to socialize.

She pulled herself out of her reverie as she realized that the instructor's question had spawned a rather heated conversation.

"But the colonies didn't owe America anything by that time, and England just saw them as a cash cow to be exploited. They didn't even have representation in the government."

"That's not true. England had invested money for over a century, and was still investing money in the colonies. The French and Indian war was only just over."

The instructor seemed to have taken a step back to watch excitement as two men her own age argued.

"A war of imperialist aggression between two European powers that the colonists got dragged into!' said the first speaker. He was a solidly built fellow with thick brown hair and an open, expressive face. She considered him cute, but had never had occasion to talk to him before.

"A war in which the colonies pressured England to protect them! And as for representation, almost no one had direct representation, even back in England." The other was the class know-it all, a fellow who tried to answer every question the teacher asked. She didn't think nearly as much of him.

"Oh, don't even argue 'virtual representation'. What a scam. It's almost as bad as our own colonies, who are 'represented' by a corporation controlled by the military. The vote back in England was almost completely based on land ownership, and most of the colonists did own land, yet they still didn't have representatives, and couldn't vote in elections."

"That may be, although I think you're making too big a deal out of it, but the fact remains that the colonies cost a fortune to run and never would have been set up to begin with if the mother country didn't think it would make its money back. The colonists knew that before they ever shipped out. Just like colonists today."

"Who asked them to keep spending money? The colonists would be just fine on their own. Give us a few years without interference and we could pay back everything we supposedly 'owe' ".

Linda fidgeted. She wanted to cut in on the discussion, but it was veering perilously close to topics that she wasn't supposed to discuss in public. Of course, the prohibition mostly applied to the media; she had been quite good about not talking to reporters, especially since the press conference. Mark had not mentioned anything about talking to ordinary civilians, yet she had got the sense he would have been happier if she had not talked to anyone at all. But she hadn't realized that the cute guy was a colonial, and she tended to agree with his points. She was getting ready to interject when the teacher finally shut the discussion down,

"Good points, both of you. Back them up with concrete examples and develop your arguments and I'll give you both A's on the test. But we need to move on because I have some other questions for you to discuss..."

When the class finished Linda followed the colonial boy out the door and swung in next to him as he walked down the hallway. "Hi, I'm Linda. I really thought you made some good points on that American Independence stuff."

"You think so? Thanks. Sometimes I get annoyed that no one sees history repeating. Maybe it's because I'm usually the only colonial around here. I'm Brett, by the way."

"I'm a colonial too. From Morning Glory. Which planet are you from?"

"Jackpot. Isn't Morning Glory the colony they just found again? I heard you had it pretty rough."

"I'm the only survivor. I heard Jackpot did fine without Earth."

"Just luck. We had a good resource base and were already doing some manufacturing when the Gate blew. Hey, are you doing anything right now? Want to go have some coffee?"

"Sure, I'd like that," which was true, even though she still didn't like coffee.

Linda let herself into the flat, fresh from her fourth date with Brett. At least, she thought it had been a date. She still didn't know much about courtship customs on Jackpot. For that matter, she wasn't sure she had a handle on Earth-style dating. He hadn't used the d-word. For that matter. Nor, for that matter, had he professed his undying love or even tried to kiss her. But he did seem interested. He had certainly gotten very close earlier when he had been showing her how to shoot.

It had been Brett's idea to go to the shooting range on their last date. Apparently shooting was a big deal back on Jackpot. The way he described the savanna where his family ranched, it sounded like a warmer version of Morning Glory's prairie, but the animals were apparently quite a lot bigger. She suspected that he might have played up the size and ferocity of some of the predators to impress her, but it did sound like protecting the cattle from them was more or less a full-time job. She had enjoyed learning to use a pistol, and Brett, himself an expert, had told her that she had a natural talent.

This trip, Brett had demonstrated once more that he was a master marksman. She hadn't done badly herself, either with the pistol or with the light rifle that she had rented. It had less recoil than and better sights than her crossbow, not to mention much less cranking between shots. It had been a fun day. She was even thinking of buying a rifle of her own. There had been a couple of nice ones in the shop at the range.

She wondered if Andrea would help her pick one out. She could ask Brett of course, but it would be more fun just to produce it from her luggage if she ever visited him on his home planet. She let a fantasy of hunting with Brett on Jackpot (which was always a warm sunny world, in her imagination) play through her head as she walked into the kitchen to grab a Cherry Coke.

After the range they had gone to a local cafe, where they had fallen to talking about Terrans, and their complacency. "I have nothing against them individually," Brett had told her, "but most of them waste their lives in boring jobs, where their bodies and minds get soft and weak, just so they can afford holo sets and luxury cars and other toys to make themselves even more soft and weak. And even that wouldn't bother me, except every one of them thinks their lifestyle is better than ours in the colonies, and either pities us or thinks we're ungrateful for all the 'help' they give us."

"Andrea and her people aren't soft or weak." she had said, which was certainly true. Even the Marines assigned to the Gate Compound, however, although they were all fit and, according to Andrea, fully qualified to fight, seemed to mostly have technical or administrative jobs. Only Andrea's special platoon were full-time scouts and fighters.

"They're the exceptions. Most of them would do well out in the colonies, if they weren't here risking their lives for people who've never even gone through the Gate."

"And yet," she had observed, "here we both are, living on their planet, eating at one of their restaurants, and going to one of their colleges."

"That's true, but we'll have all that, and sooner than they think. Will our kids bother coming to Earth? Earth's the past. We're the future."

She hadn't really disagreed with him, and actually admired his passion. Earth was...an experience, and it was certainly better than being all alone on Morning Glory, but she thought she would probably get tired of it and head back out to the colonies in a few years.

As Linda turned back from the fridge, soft drink in hand, she noticed that her phone was blinking. It was a recent purchase, and she hadn't gotten used to carrying it with her constantly the way Terrans did. She had conveniently "forgotten" it earlier, not wanting to be interrupted with Brett. She wondered who had called her and left a message.

A glance at the display showed that the call had come from the Marine battalion offices at the Gate Complex. There was no voice message, just four words of text, "Call HQ ASAP – Singh." It was the first time the Colonel had ever contacted her directly, and she hadn't spoken with him at all in weeks.

She thumbed the call-back command and was surprised when she heard Andrea's voice rather than that of the clerk who normally directed calls.

"Linda? Where are you? We need you to come in right away."

"Why? What's going on?"

"I don't want to talk specifics over a civilian connection. Let's just say your mother just came into town."

Chapter 6

AMY KEPT HER EYES CLOSED and tried to wait out the headache. Aohrs claimed the hibernation capsule was in perfect working order, but its deactivation protocol seemed a little rough on humans...or whatever she was now. Still, it was apparently a lot easier on the sentient brain than the discordant non-Euclidean hell that was hyperspace. And the fact that Aohrs himself had survived in one for the better part of sixteen centuries (even if his companion had been less lucky) argued for its reliability.

She opened her eyes in time to see Aohrs disappear up a ladder, on his way to the bridge to try to figure out where they were this time. As they had prearranged, she stayed and checked their capsules. They couldn't take the reliability of 1,600-year-old (give or take) equipment for granted, and they might need to leave in a hurry. They should have had at least two additional crew members doing their own checklists in engineering. Given the circumstances, though, they had to rely on the computers to do what they thought best back there. Aohrs had been the equivalent of a medic before long term hibernation had robbed him of large chunks of his memory, and Amy was a biologist who could barely read the language used by the ship's computers—if either of them tried to mess with the ships engines they were more likely to break something than help.

She finished her checklist and permitted herself to stretch luxuriously. Her bones no longer moved quite the same way as they had when she was a human, but her back still got stiff. Then she climbed to the bridge to see if Aorhs needed help.

This was...she had to think about it...the fifth star they had visited. She hoped it would at least offer a chance to restock their dwindling supply of meat (kept in one of the extra hibernation capsules, of course). Better yet would be if it offered a trail back to either humanity or Aorhs' people, the Mersphi. Although either would be an improvement over wondering the depths of space until their antique ship broke down, she would prefer humanity. While she had only a dim idea of how much time had passed back on Terra—subjectively, she had only been awake for a few months since her change—she was fairly sure that there would still be people there who had known her when she was human, and who would help her send a rescue party to get Jim, Linda and Mary off Morning Glory. The same was almost certainly not true for Aorhs.

So far, though, they were lost.

The problem, as she understood it, was the topology of hyperspace, which was radically different from that of normal space. The "next star over" from the perspective of a ship like this might be hundreds of parsecs away in the real world. From what they could glean from the ship's library, hyperspace astrogation, once off the established trade lanes, had been about thirty-percent advanced calculus and seventy-percent seat-of-the-pants scientific guessing, and all the reference books were in a notation that they were just now beginning to understand. So knowing where Morning Glory was in relation to Earth in normal space (which she did, if only in approximate terms) wasn't much help. At least not unless they wanted to just point the ship in normal space and cold-sleep it—which would work as long as the ship didn't break down, but wouldn't get them there in time to help anyone.

Luckily, she had somehow managed to hold on to her portable comp when they had left Morning Glory. Even more luckily, it contained a children's book on astronomy, originally intended for Linda when she got older, which showed the positions of several bright stars in relation to Sol and the larger colonies. This information, laboriously hand-input into the astrogation computer, should at least allow them to know when they were near human space. And a program on the computer that she thought she understood should provide a mapping function for a course for the final jump to Sol, but only if they could get close enough.

"Jackpot!" said Aohrs. His English had been getting better rapidly.

"We're in the Jackpot System! That's terrific."

"No, not at Jackpot. We hit a jackpot. I wish humans were more careful about naming things, it would save confusion."

"What do you mean?"

"I mean, if you used certain words for names and others for colloquialisms it would..."

"No, I mean what jackpot did we hit?"

"This system contains a large orbital habitat which was not here last time the ship visited. Also, the computer has found three stars which it is ninety-five percent confident are shown on your human space star pictures. Conclusion: this is a human habitat."

Amy let out a cheer, then slipped in front of the communication console and began transmitting on what, according to her calculations, should be the human in-system hailing frequency. Hours later, though, after trying other frequencies and transmission modes, she was forced to conclude that no one on the other side was going to answer. In fact, there didn't seem to be any artificial radio chatter in the system at all.

"No dice, Aorhs."

He stared at her blankly.

"I mean, still no answer. I think it must be abandoned. Do you think it's worth docking and seeing what's up?"

"Almost certainly. But the ship's automatic docking procedures will not work on a human station. Are you able to dock us?" The ship's controls had a simulation mode, and they had both practiced manual docking. Amy was better at it, but that wasn't saying much.

"Probably not. I can get us in the same orbit, though, if we want to EVA. Do we have any suits?"

"I believe so. I will look while you bring us in. That way I won't have to watch you drive."

There were three suits that seemed operational. Mersphi vacuum suits looked quite similar to the Terran equivalent; yet another instance of form following function.

"There's no need for both of us to go," she told her alien companion, "if it's a human habitat I should be the one."

"Are you sure?"

"Just show me how to get this thing on and off. Then stay here by the com in case I need help."

The suit's fastenings and controls were simple and obvious, the result of a long design evolution. She mistrusted the plumbing connections, though, and opted not to hook them up. Some things were just too alien.

She listened to the pounding of her own heart as the airlock lost pressure, then swung open. Although the Colonial Administration operated both planetary colonies and space habitats, she had been on the dirt-side career track. This was her first space walk.

With the door open she could clearly see the side of the habitat, a torus of ceramic and synthetics at least three times as big as the ship. The airlock she was aiming for was emblazoned with plenty of bright orange paint, and she was sure the hull of the habitat would be liberally supplied with grab handles. She just needed to get there and she ought to have no problem making her way along the outside. Checking the aerosol can and magnetic grapple on their lanyards she climbed out the airlock, aimed as well as she could, and kicked off gently.

She knew that experienced spacers could flip themselves in mid flight, landing like a cat with their boots against the target. She tried no such maneuvers. At the slow speed she was drifting she could simply run into the wall and grab something.

Halfway across the span she began considering whether to apply a course correction with the spray can at her belt. She was going to hit the habitat, but not very close to the airlock she wanted. She had just reached down to take up the slack in the lanyard when she heard a loud ripping sound and watched the right forearm of her suit blow off into space as the ancient glue in the elbow joint gave way.

"Aahh!" she yelled, but it was taken away as all the air rushed out of the suit before the automatic tourniquet closed in the shoulder joint. At least that still worked. Out of the corner of her eye she saw her right hand expanding, already coated with frost rime. It hurt. A lot.

"Amy," the radio cracked, "what is your status?"

"Hang on Aorhs," she wheezed, "little busy here."

The reaction from the escaping gauntlet and air had sent her into a spin and knocked her off course. She scrambled for the aerosol can with her left hand, finally raising it into position. She was retching, trying not to puke from the erratic motion and the pain.

Her first air blast seemed to make her spin worse. She took a deep breath and tried again. This time, while she was still spinning, she seemed to be headed back towards the station. She dropped the still tethered spray can and fished up the grapple. She waited until she thought she was close enough then, when the spin took her around, pushed the trigger on the spring launcher, sending the magnet head towards the station, where it dragged then caught.

It took an eternity to awkwardly pull in the thin line of the grapple using only one arm. Why hadn't the Mersphi thought to build in some kind of electric winch? Finally, she thudded into the hull in a tangle of line, breaking off her now frozen and brittle right hand in the process. At least that didn't make it hurt any worse than it already had.

Finally she made it to an airlock (possibly even the one she had started for), flipped up the protective cover over the controls, and punched the "open" button. She managed to climb in against the slight gravity created by the station's spin and cycle through the lock before tearing off her helmet and vomiting on the floor. Only later did it occur to her that she should probably have first made sure the station had breathable air.

She collapsed on the deck next to her helmet and spoke into it, "I'm here, Aorhs."

"What is happening?"

"Your piece-of-crap spacesuit blew out. I lost an arm."

"I apologize."

"You'd better. If I was still human it would be a big deal!" she began laughing hysterically. As usual, he did not join in.

Her now useless vacuum suit stripped off, and somewhat cleaned up, Amy moved through the halls of the station, occasionally scratching at the itchy nubbin of flesh which would soon be a new right forearm. The hallways were colder and darker than they should be and the air tasted a bit stale. She passed a hatch that was marked as the station commander's office and kept going. She would return later, but for now she needed food, especially protein. Locating the galley she found a container of the Colonial Administration's ubiquitous protein powder and started eating it by the spoonful. It wasn't what she craved—which was raw meat and lots of it—but it should keep her from going into shock.

Once her initial need abated she paused to glance into the storage lockers and deep freeze, which were mostly about a third full. Whatever had caused this station to be abandoned, the inhabitants hadn't starved like the people of Morning Glory. She wondered if she would be able to transfer some of the food back to the ship. It probably wouldn't be worth it, though; the Colonial Administration's standard diet wasn't much use to obligate carnivores.

Taking the rest of the canister of powder with her, she walked (or rather glided in the low gravity) back towards the commander's office.

The office was locked, of course, but it was a normal door, not a pressure hatch, so she broke the latch easily with her left hand.

The computer access built into the narrow desk yielded itself to her colonial login and she began skimming those log entries which were accessible at her user level. From what she could glean, this colony was named Thule-B and it was just about the furthest point from Sol to which humans had had Gate access. The plan had been to build a new railgun here and begin launching probes to expand the human perimeter even further. From what she could tell, though, the habitat itself had barely been completed—was actually still being worked on here and there, and the railgun and its attendant probe manufactory had not even begun operations when the Gate had stopped opening.

The habitat had had working hydroponics and, although the last few logs complained that spare parts for equipment were running out, should have been able to keep going for months or even years. But the last log entries ran out only a few weeks after the Gate failure. Had some key component failed, killing everyone despite whatever fail-safes were in place? If so, where were the bodies and why was life support still up, albeit at barely adequate levels?

She stood up from the desk, pushing the chair in with her now complete right hand and began looking for the station's Gate landing. Upon finding it she flipped on the computer in the booth and found her answer: a log made by Terran Marines when they had gated into a station that had become a carbon dioxide choked death trap after the last life-support micro-controller had shorted out. The Marines, apparently, had cleaned up the bodies and replaced the board, then updated the log per regulations and gone on their way. There was no explanation of why the Gate had failed, nor mention of when, or if, anyone planned to return here. But at least the Gate was functioning again somewhere. That meant Morning Glory might already have been relieved.

She used the Gate desk's com interface to call Aohrs, who answered immediately. It was a relief to confirm that human and Mersphi radio equipment could actually interoperate. She told him what she had learned.

"I'll be back in an hour or two. I just need to find a new vac suit...and check it very carefully."

Signing off, she keyed the panel to take voice dictation and began narrating her own log entry, not sure if anyone would ever hear it.

Chapter 7

MY NAME IS DR. AMY Ott-Harris and I am the chief biologist of the Morning Glory colony. The way I got here is quite a story, and you may not believe most of it, but I think I had better just tell the whole thing and let you draw your own conclusions. If all goes well I will be on Earth myself anyway before anyone ever reads this.

Everything started when our Gate stopped opening. You probably know about that. From what I've seen here, lots of peoples' Gates stopped opening. Morning Glory was a new colony and we were already on short rations because we hadn't managed to grow our own food yet. After the supply line was cut we starved and things got...really bad. Martial law, fighting in the streets, even cannibalism. If you can, you need to send a rescue party right away. And be sure not to look just in the town. Some of the colonists went to hide in the hills. My husband and daughter should still be hiding in the hills.

I'm not with them because around eighteen weeks after the Gate failed, I encountered an alien life-form and he...transformed me, for lack of a better word. I was dying of an injury inflicted by another colonist and he infected me with what we now know are very advanced nanites, just as he had been infected by a third race in a different system. I've studied my blood samples and his and these are incredible; hundreds of years beyond anything we can make on earth. They don't just speed healing, they make me stronger and faster and increase my pain threshold and adrenaline production. To give you an idea, three hours ago I lost my right arm up to the elbow in an EVA accident. Now it has grown back good as new. As far as I know the best Terran regeneration techniques would take a month or more to do that, under hospital conditions. And it hurt like hell, but never so much I wasn't functional.

That part is all wonderful, but there are drawbacks too. As near as we can tell, the nanites permanently change the DNA of their host and then reconfigure their bodies to match. I'm still humanoid, but not human. Also, all that healing and reconfiguring takes a massive energy and protein budget. The hunger for fresh meat right afterwards is incredibly intense. And while it is possible to control who or what I infect with the nanites now, I couldn't at first. That's how they spread: newly infected individuals infect most prey animals that they don't manage to kill outright. A whole ecosystem can wind up filled with nothing but super predators overnight and collapse. That's what seems to have happened to Morning Glory before humans got there.

My companion, Aohrs, and I have talked about several theories of where the nanites came from. He's a medic so he has a pretty good background in the Mersphi's—that's his race's—life sciences. Anyway, one possibility is that the whole thing is a bioweapon, but we think that's unlikely. As a way to destroy a biosphere it is much too complicated to make sense. Additionally, only a fool would give their enemies super strength if they could help it.

Aohrs thinks that the nanites were designed to adapt colonists for harsh environments but something went wrong, allowing them to transfer to other species. I guess that's actually pretty plausible.

Equally plausible, though, is that we are looking at some sort of super soldier program by an aggressive race—a race that might still be out there. If so, they've had a minimum of sixteen centuries since then to improve the nanite technology, which is a pretty scary thought.

Anyway, Aohrs and I have a faster than light ship and we are trying to get to Earth. Like I said, I might be there before anyone reads this. But if you are reading this, and you haven't heard from me, then try to get help to Morning Glory.

Ott-Harris out.

Amy date-sealed the file and signed it biometrically, then set it to play automatically the first time someone accessed the console or to upload to any message beacon that came through. Then she went looking for a good suit to return to the ship. They would need to find a planet to hunt on soon, but then they could continue looking for Earth. And they would find their way back, even if it took years.

Chapter 8

SEARGEANT LI WAS WAITING for Linda at the guard post when she arrived.

"What the heck is going on?" she asked, as she pinned on the visitor badge he handed her.

"I have no idea, which means it's probably way above my pay grade. They just told me to wait for you and bring you to the colonel. The lieutenant is already there with him at the command post."

She followed Li to an elevator that brought them to a much lower level than she had ever been allowed to visit before. From the elevator lobby they passed through a set of massive steel doors (currently open) into a room where half a dozen Marine NCOs with headsets sat watching dozens of monitors with disciplined intent. Colonel Singh paced in the middle of the room while Andrea Hardy and Captain Leiber, his intelligence officer, tried to stay out of his path. He spun to face Linda, dismissing Li with a wave of his hand.

"Ms. Harris, sorry to disturb you, but we have a situation and you may be able to help us. You may not be aware, but Earth has an early warning system designed to spot dangerous objects. For the past nineteen hours it had been tracking a small but very fast moving object that is on an exact course for Earth.

"Normally that wouldn't be our concern—neither the Marines nor the Gate Corp. Space Force would wait until it got into optimal range and blast it into small pieces with orbital weapons. About two hours ago, though, it started transmitting—in English— and we realized it was a ship, even though it's going faster than any of our ships normally go and it's on a vector where no Terran ship has any business being.

"Of course it would still be Space Force's problem, except that the message specifically asks for Gate HQ so they decided to patch us in.

"Play the message," he ordered. One of the technicians typed a quick key sequence.

"Starship Rah'ktll to Earth Gate Headquarters, if that still exists. This is Dr. Amy Ott-Harris, chief biologist from the Morning Glory colony. Morning Glory is cut off from the Gate network and in urgent need of relief. Things were...really bad there when we left. Please, I need to speak to a senior Gate Corporation or Colonial Administration official."

"Andrea was right," mumbled Linda, "my mother *is* back in town."

Colonel Singh shot Hardy a look that said she probably shouldn't have let slip even that much over the phone.

"The message repeats on a loop," added Captain Leiber, "ordinary FM signal, wide beam, on a standard working frequency. The entire inner system is probably hearing it."

"Has anyone answered?" asked Linda.

"Orbital Control challenged them and ordered them to dump velocity as soon as they got the first transmission," answered the captain, "No response, and their speed hasn't changed."

"So we have a problem," said Singh, "and that's why I called you here Ms. Harris. There are two questions we need to answer: First, is that actually your mother, or is it a piece of space junk launched at us by terrorists with a recording to keep us from blasting it? Second, if it is your mother, is she here on her own, or with an alien invasion force?"

"I don't know about the first question, Colonel. I haven't heard my mother's voice since I was a toddler. That might be her, but I can't tell you for sure. As for the second part, even if she's alone she's dangerous. She isn't human any more. Carmen was sneaky and cunning enough, but my Mother was smarter than her to begin with. You can't trust anyone who's been infected by these aliens."

"Status change, Sirs," reported one of the techs, "OC reports the bogie is braking now. They note that the delta-*v* is off the scale. The *g*-forces on that ship must be tremendous."

"Hmm," mused Singh, "that makes the first possibility less likely. I suppose I'd better talk to her and see what she wants. Sergeant, open a channel."

Singh put on an extra headset. As soon as the sergeant nodded he began to speak.

"Alien vessel, this is Lieutenant Colonel Vijay Singh, Terran Marine Corps. I'm chief of security for the Gate Corporation. We have received your message but the Morning Glory colony has already been relieved. Please explain how you acquired this ship and what your immediate intentions are." He turned off the microphone. "What's the turn-around time?"

"About eight minutes, Sir, but getting shorter faster."

"Colonel," said a different tech, "OC just sent us some calculations they did. If this is right, then that ship is impossible."

"It can't be impossible, Marine, since it's here now."

"That's not what I mean, Sir. I mean that there shouldn't be any way it can generate that much delta-*v*. Not with any known space drive system. And as far as we can tell, it's not shooting any reaction mass either."

"Meaning what?"

"We are dealing with a reactionless drive, driven by a power plant that our technology can't even imagine. This is strictly space opera stuff, Colonel. And that can't be their main drive, either. Even a drive like that can't exceed the speed of light, so the fact that they got here this fast means that they also have a way to go faster than light."

"Some new application of Gate technology?"

"Sir, I really have no idea."

"Message coming in, Sir," the tech at the communications console broke in.

"Play it."

"Please, I'll explain everything," said the voice of Amy Ott-Harris, "but you need to tell me if my husband and daughter got off Morning Glory. I...I need to know." There was an indrawing of breath, audible over the microphone, as she collected herself, "My companion Aorhs is a member of the alien race that built this vessel. He made contact with my family and I several weeks after the Gate had broken down. After I lost contact with the rest of my party, Aorhs led me back to his ship, which we were able to launch in the hopes of contacting Terrans and requesting aid for Morning Glory. It took us a lot longer to get to Earth than we thought it would."

"Ms. Harris," said Colonel Singh, "does that story check out with what you were told?"

"As far as I can tell, Colonel. Mary and my parents did meet someone named Aorhs, who seemed to be the same kind of creature as Carmen turned into. My mother did leave with him after he healed her injuries. We never saw either of them again, so maybe they left the planet. She isn't saying anything about the alien gene virus, though."

"Yes, I noticed that." He keyed his microphone back on. "Dr. Ott-Harris I need you to assume an orbit which Orbital Control will be sending you shortly, then shut down all of your systems except communications and basic life support. Then we will discuss how to proceed from there. I can tell you, though, that your daughter Linda survived and is present right now at Gate Headquarters."

He thumbed off his microphone. "Mute that channel and give me whoever is in command at Orbital Control," a moment later he replied to someone whom he could hear over his headset, "Yes, Major, this is Colonel Singh. I am inclined to believe that the person on that ship actually is Dr. Ott-Harris, but we also have reason to believe she is infected with a dangerous alien virus. Additionally, we have no way to judge the capabilities of that ship. I have told her to expect an orbital assignment from you. I strongly suggest that you put them under as many of your guns as possible and watch closely to make sure they actually shut down their systems. I am also requesting transport for a Marine boarding party that will be gating up to you in twenty minutes," he listened to something from the other side, then, "I know, but if there's any way, any way at all to get control of that vessel I think it's our job to try."

The speaker cracked on with Amy's returning message, "Linda's there? Can you put her on? Please, let me talk to her!"

Singh looked at Hardy, who shrugged, then at Linda. "Ms. Harris," he asked, "do you want to talk to your mother? I'm still afraid she will do something erratic. Talking to you might help keep her calm."

Linda really didn't know whether she wanted to talk to Amy or not. But it seemed cowardly to refuse, so she said, "I'll talk to her."

"All right, I'll allow a short conversation. However, you are not to say anything about what you just heard me say to that officer at OC, about the orbital weapons or the boarding party which Lieutenant Hardy is now leaving to organize." Hardy spun on her heel and headed for the door.

"I understand," said Linda, and took another of the headsets from the com tech.

"Transmission delay is down to around a minute now, round trip," said the tech, "that thing really covers ground."

Linda pushed the stud to turn on the microphone, as she had watched the Colonel do. "This is Linda Harris. Is this actually my mother? And are you a human, or a space monster, or what?"

A short time later, they all heard, "Linda! Is that really you? I'm so glad to hear your voice, baby! It's been so long."

"Yes, about fifteen years. Can you please answer the question? We know all about the alien virus. You may have been my mother once, but how do we know you aren't here now to conquer the planet and try to eat us?"

"It isn't like that, Linda. It's true that the virus changes us, and at first we have trouble controlling ourselves and can be dangerous to the people around us. But that passes. Aorhs and I are completely reasonable, and we don't want to eat anyone."

"That's a load of bull-crap!" replied Linda, after the delay, using an expression she had learned from the Marines, "After Carmen caught the virus she killed dozens of people, then spent the next decade hunting down Mary and I. She never got over the virus or stopped wanting to eat humans."

"That can't be right. I killed Carmen myself. Listen, just tell the military to let us land. We have pretty good atmospheric flight capability so we can come down anywhere they tell us. They're welcome to put out as much security as they want to watch us. You'll all see that we are normal people. I really want to see you. I've been missing you all this time."

"You killed Carmen, huh? I guess that's just another thing you messed up and had to leave Mary to take care of, like raising me. I still think you're probably a space monster, and I can't say I missed you at all. But I'll still give you some advice: get the hell out of Earth-space while you can. They're going to board your ship and take it, and I wouldn't care, except they'll use it against decent colonials like you used to be. So leave now while..."

Singh ripped the headset off of her while the tech scrambled to complete the circuit. After the delay they heard Amy calling Linda's name, her voice rising in pitch as she became increasingly worried and frustrated.

"Sir," said the sergeant, "OC reports that the ship is accelerating. It looks like they are setting up a hyperbolic course away from Earth."

Linda felt very small and defenseless as Singh loomed over her, his face displaying more emotion that she had ever seen there. "What were you thinking? Do you have any idea what you might have done? That little stunt could have made them nuke the whole planet, or whatever they have that passes for nukes. Why would you even do that?" Linda wondered if she was supposed to answer any of those questions, but he didn't seem to be giving her the chance. "It was my fault," he said, already growing calmer, "I don't know what I was thinking, putting a damn fool brainless teenage girl on the com during a situation like this. I'll tell you one thing, though, if you were one of my Marines you would be up on charges and headed to the brig right now." He took a deep breath, "but you're a civilian, and I don't have time right now to figure out what civilian laws you've broken. So go straight home to your apartment and stay there under house arrest until I tell you you can leave. Don't talk to anyone, and I mean anyone. Go. Now." He pointed towards the door.

Linda slunk down the corridors towards the exit, hoping she had done the right thing. She had had no idea what she was going to say until she had said it. But it had been clear enough to her that the military wanted the ship. And if they had it it would be one more advantage they had that they would use to try to force the colonials into line. And if they couldn't get it, they would have destroyed it to keep anyone else from getting it. And what if they had fouled things up and let the monsters onto the planet? Let her mother onto the planet...

She had actually been talking to her mother! All these years, she had been so sure that her mother was dead, or at least gone forever. That had been bad, but it was something she could understand, even when she was young. After all, her dad and Mary's wife, and nearly everyone else on the planet were also dead. Yeah, she had known death her entire life. You shot a gopher and it stopped moving and went stiff. Then you ate it for dinner. No more gopher. If Carmen caught a person, pretty much the same thing happened. Death was just something you lived with every day.

A live mother was much harder to deal with. A mother who sat up in an incredible spaceship that could probably wipe out the planet, talking like a nice lady, when actually you knew she was a human-eating space monster? How was anyone supposed to deal with that?

She realized that she might have made a massive mistake. Instead of scaring Amy's ship away, maybe instead she should have found an excuse to get Singh to blast it. She didn't know what she should have done. She didn't know what was going to happen to her now. Would they put her in jail? Or maybe they would just shove her in a Gate back to Morning Glory and tell her not to ever come back. She had never seen Singh get mad like that.

She realized that she had reached the front door of the apartment, despite not remembering any of the walk over. She keyed her code into the lock and went in.

The apartment was empty, of course. Even though she wouldn't be leading a boarding party now, it would probably be hours before Andrea could stand down and come home. That might be just as well. She wanted to talk to someone (imagine that, for a girl who had lived completely alone for six years!) but she wasn't sure that Andrea wouldn't feel the same way as Singh. Still, if there were anyone to whom Singh's orders not to talk to anyone did not apply, it would be Andrea Hardy, leader of the special recon platoon.

She sat down by the holo and began flipping channels. One news show had a story about an asteroid passing near Earth that had been determined by Orbital Control to not pose a threat to the planet nor shipping. She idly wondered whether all of the Terran news stories had about the same proportion of truth in them. How did they expect to keep things hushed, after so many people had heard the radio conversation? She was too restless to stay on any channel for long, and soon turned off the set.

She only had one friend who wasn't in the Marine Corps, and he was also the only one likely to understand why she had refused to let that starship fall into Terran hands. She wasn't sure it was right to involve him, and she probably shouldn't ignore Colonel Singh's orders, but she felt like she was going to go insane if she didn't talk to someone. She picked up her phone and sent a message to Brett.

He was there within fifteen minutes. Despite all of the chaos in her head, she allowed herself to feel pleased that he had thought this was important enough—that she was important enough—to drop whatever he had been doing and come over. As soon as he was through the front door she began pouring out the whole story. He stopped her with an upraised hand, then began pointing towards the door and pantomiming a person's walking legs with two fingers.

"I can't leave," she said, "I'm under house arrest."

He made a shushing gesture with his fingers, then pointed at her, then himself, then made the walking motion again. She shook her head and pointed to the floor at her feet, trying to convey that they should stay where they were.

He took out his phone and input some text, then turned it so she could read: *dont talk here. apt maybe bugged*

As soon as he was sure she had read it he cleared the text. She took the phone from him and typed: *whats bugged mean?*

He took the phone and replied: *listening devices. electronic. come with me.* Instead of waiting for a reply he took her hand and gently pulled her towards the door. She let herself be pulled. *How about that,* she thought, *it's the first time we've held hands.*

Brett didn't release her until they had arrived at a small park at the end of the block.

"Sorry," he said, "I didn't want to talk there, this is too important."

"Do you actually think Colonel Singh would spy on us? That doesn't seem like his style. He just doesn't seem that paranoid."

"I'm not worried about Singh. Or not very worried, anyway. He is really just security. He's there to handle visible threats and to reassure the public that the military is on the job. There are other people watching the Gate Corporation who don't advertise their presence and who love to spy on people. They probably even spy on Singh."

"I never thought of that. Which group is in charge?"

"Not Singh, although he might think he is."

"Ugh. Everything on this planet is so complicated."

"No kidding. So, we left in a hurry, but what I understood from you is that your mother showed up in a spaceship and you told her to get lost and not deal with the Terrans. I thought you said your mother died just after the Gate failure."

"We thought she had. Uh, the whole story is a little more complicated than I told you. I didn't know you that well yet when I told you about my mother, and I'm still not sure you'll believe me."

"Try me. I mean, you just believed me when I told you that parties unknown were bugging your apartment, so I owe you one. Let's talk as we walk, though. We're too easy to find if we stay in one place, and they have devices to listen outside from a distance, too."

As they walked she told him the entire story, including the parts Mary had told her from before she was old enough to remember clearly. "So that's it," she finished, "I don't trust Mom or this Aorhs person, and I don't trust the Terrans with this crazy-advanced technology, or with the space virus. They're already trying to clamp down on the colonies. If they had ships like that and they could make as many alien-vampire-monsters as they wanted then we wouldn't have any chance at all."

"You say 'we'. Do you feel that you are a colonial? One hundred percent, I mean, with no ambiguity?"

"That's a really strange way to put it. Of course I have some ambiguity. Most of my friends are Terran, and they're not bad people. But if trouble's coming and I have to pick a side, then of course I'm with the colonials. I lived on a colony my entire life. I was raised by a woman who had worked in the colonies most of her life. Most of my inheritance, if they ever let me have it, is land in the colonies, and I'll probably go back out there as soon as I get enough education to be useful. So yeah, I know which side I'm on. I think I already proved it once today."

"That's what I was sure you would say, but I had to hear it. The fact is, I simplified my story a bit too. Everything I told you about growing up on a ranch on Jackpot, and about coming here for college is true. But I didn't tell you that my father is more than just a rancher. He's one of the main leaders in the movement that wants more autonomy for the colonies. He and I are both in the Jackpot Militia, which you've probably never heard of because the Terrans like to pretend we don't exist. But we do exist, and we'll fight to protect our freedom and our homes. Also, even though I really am here to go to college, I have orders to keep my eye on the Gate and I send home regular reports. It is no coincidence that I applied to a college right here, where a bunch of the Marines in the security detachment just happen to take classes." He stopped talking and looked at her hesitantly, as if unsure how she would respond.

"I think I respect you even more than I already did."

"Thanks. That actually means a lot to me."

They didn't talk for the next two blocks. She noticed that her hand was somehow in his again.

Finally, he broke the silence. "I've been thinking about your story. I know what you said about Carmen being psychotic and killing everyone, but it sounds like your mother was actually acting pretty reasonable, considering the situation. And according to your foster mother, didn't Aorhs actually infect her with the virus because it was the only way to save her life? What if Carmen was an exception, and this virus doesn't automatically make people crazy?"

"It does at first. My mom had to take herself away from us. And today on the radio she said that they have trouble controlling themselves right after they get infected."

"Okay, granted. But your mother has had years now to get control. I'm curious, what was Carmen like before she got infected?"

"I was too young to know. According to Mary she was sneaky and selfish. But Mary wasn't exactly an impartial witness. Mary said that Carmen basically led the mob that killed Masami and injured my Mom, when we were all trying to get out of town."

"Okay. And you said that lots of the colonists had turned to cannibalism, even before Carmen got infected."

"Yeah. That's why my parents decided to get out of town when they did."

"So what if Carmen was basically acting the way she would have anyway, and the virus just let her do it more effectively?"

"Maybe a little. But you didn't live all those years with Carmen hunting you. She thought like a monster, not a human. She was also really good at setting traps and ambushes. I just can't know that my Mother isn't doing the same."

"Alright. But what if your mother is sane? Wouldn't she sympathize with the colonies, the same as you and for the same reasons?"

"Speaking hypothetically? Yeah, I guess so. Are you thinking of trying to get in touch with her? It's too late. She's gone."

"It was just a thought. Never mind, we have more immediate problems. Basically, I would advise you against staying on Terra any longer. If they decide you're a problem for them then you won't be safe."

"Do you really think I'm in that much danger?"

"Yes. I do."

"Well, even if that's true, how am I supposed to get off Earth? There's only one Gate, and they own it."

"What if I told you there is a way to get off of Earth and back out to the colonies? Today. I'm absolutely serious. Would you let me take you?"

She thought about it. She had told him the truth when she had said she was planning to go back to the colonies, but she had planned to stay on Earth long enough to straighten out her inheritance and earn some sort of marketable technical certification. Probably another three years, at least. And how did he plan to get them off the planet, unless he had...

"Another Gate?"

He grinned. "So what's your answer? I did promise to show you around Jackpot, after all."

Part 3 - Human Confederation
Chapter 9

THE OUTGOING LANDING for Brett's Gate more than brought back memories of the landing on Morning Glory, located as it was in a seemingly abandoned warehouse in a run-down neighborhood. Unlike the other Gate Landings Linda had seen, however, it had no safety ropes and no control booth with equipment to log shipments and route message traffic. All that marked the pad itself was a spray-painted rectangle on the concrete that looked like it had been there forever. They stood in the center of the rectangle as the clock on Brett's wrist comp counted down and translated smoothly at the scheduled time, arriving in afternoon sunlight on the asphalt in front of a large log structure.

Two older men covered the landing with large-bore shotguns. As soon as they recognized Brett, however, they slung their weapons and nodded to him in friendly recognition.

"Hi Bill, Vern. Anything new?" Brett asked.

"Same-oh, same-oh Brett—I mean Lieutenant. Gate duty isn't much different, at this end, whether it's our Gate or theirs."

"Hell, Vern. Just call me Brett. It's not like a shooting war has started yet?" his tone was jocular, but the end of the sentence trailed up in a question mark.

"No change yet, Brett."

"Well, hang in there. Things are bound to get interesting at some point."

Ultimately, few of humanity's planets had ever lived up to the fanciful names assigned to them by the Colonial Administration. Jackpot, however, was an exception. It had a climate similar to Terra's in the mid-Pleistocene, with timber for building, good sites for wind and hydroelectric power, and numerous edible herd animals, some of which were prospects for domestication. The local predators, while large and fierce, were no match for the colonists' modern firearms. Most of the standard food crops adapted with a minimum of genetic tinkering. With these advantages, Jackpot had advanced quickly beyond the subsistence stage and began importing the equipment it needed for a sustainable tech base, trading hardwood and other products that were now almost unobtainable on Terra. By the time the Gate had been destroyed Jackpot had had a population of nearly one-hundred-and-seventy-thousand, spread between one large town and numerous ranches and logging camps, and had been a going concern long enough for many of the children of the original colonists to return from the technical schools of Terra, ready to take their places in a small but expanding light industrial sector.

Linda and Brett arrived at Jackpot City to find it converted into an armed camp, complete with watch towers and sandbagged redoubts. More armed men, who had been watching to see if they would need to back the two at the Gate, snapped the safety flaps down on their holsters and went back to their work, stacking sacks of something on empty pallets.

Brett leaned against the hood of a parked jeep: a local model, clunky but serviceable. A platoon of locals marched by. They didn't wear uniforms and made no particular effort to stay in step but they had the same air of rugged competence she found so appealing in Brett himself, and each carried a rifle as if it was part of his arm.

"See that?" Brett pointed at the men and women going by, "anyone who tries to gate in a squad of troopers is going to have a fight on his hands. And unless their Gate has more capacity than they've ever shown, they won't be able to bring in more than that at once, until the capacitors recharge."

"But can't they stage them somewhere else on the planet and come at you all at once?"

"Sure, but then they need to walk across the planet to get to us, and we live here. Most of us have been out hunting in this country since we were nine or ten. Fighting them in the field would be the best thing that could happen, from our point of view, assuming the ultracrocs and direbogles didn't get them first. Anyway, the further away from their landing they send them, the worse their targeting is going to be. It would serve them right if they gated straight into a mountain.

"Not that we actually want to fight them, you understand. We just want to live on our own planet and be left alone."

Linda nodded and thought of Mary. No one knew better than her how tough colonists could be when they were forced to fight. Even so, she thought of Andrea Hardy's platoon—all too likely to be the first ones through the Gate in an invasion—with their well trained confidence and heavy body armor, and wondered if Brett was right to be so confident. She hoped it never came to that and that no one on either side got hurt. Her sympathies were unquestionably with the colonists, but some of the Marines were her friends. Andrea was her best female friend.

"Here," said Brett, "now that we're off Terra there isn't really any need to hurry, so let's sit down for a bit." He walked across the road into an opening between two buildings with several wooden tables in it. "Go ahead and sit down anywhere," he said, "I'll get us some sodas or something."

He returned shortly with two glass mugs full of brown liquid. He handed one to Linda and watched as she shipped tentatively. Sweet and bubbly, it was definitely a soft drink. The flavor, though, was unlike anything she had encountered: more complex and botanical than any of the Terran sodas she had tried. "What is this?" she asked, "It's pretty good."

"That," he explained proudly, "is Jackpot-style sarsaparilla, brewed a few blocks from here, using a root that grows all over the savanna. The mug it's in is made of locally blown glass made from local sand. I hear they can make any shape they want now, and are working up to bigger pieces," he waved his hand expansively, taking in the whole street around them, "Pretty much everything you can see from here was made locally, after the Gate failure."

"I'm impressed. While you were doing that my people were killing and eating one another."

His face darkened. "I'm sorry, I didn't mean it like that."

"I know. Don't worry, I learned to live with what happened on Morning Glory a long time ago. I'm really impressed by you guys, though. Are other colonies like this?"

"Well, Jackpot is special. New Dream is almost as developed as we are, but their climate is a lot more active, which is slowing them down. There aren't many spots on New Dream where you could have an open-air restaurant like this. They do have some terrific mineral deposits, though, right near the colony. Once the troubles are over we may build a second, dedicated, Gate, just to trade our meat and leather for their ore. Cornucopia is pretty primitive, but they have the most population of any of us; once they catch up technologically they'll be a powerhouse.

"The other colonies aren't as far along. But thirty-eight total were cut off in the Gate failure, and survived on their own. Sorry, thirty-nine, counting Morning Glory. That was the big stress test. It proves they can make it on their own. We all just need to get out from under the Colonial Administration, which sets all the Gate fees and the prices for things from Terra, and tries to tells us which things to grow and mine for their benefit, not ours."

"Mary told me that my mother wanted them to switch to hydroponics on Morning Glory at the very start, after the first crop failed, but they made us plant two more crops. And when they did send hydro units, they only sent a few."

"That's because hydroponics is an expensive way to grow food. They want the colonies to feed themselves cheaply, so they break-even sooner and start earning a profit."

"So," she asked, "does that mean that you guys want to cut contact with Terra completely?"

"Wouldn't that be better than being serfs? That isn't the goal any more, though. We have a Gate now, and New Dream is working on one, using plans we gave them. With three operating Gates colonials will be able to shop around for the best price to buy and sell. In the long run all that trade will be good for everyone, probably even Terra."

"But you don't think they'll let you. That's why you're keeping your own Gate secret, and you have armed men patrolling your streets."

"We think that if they find out about our Gate they'll use as much force as they need to to either shut it down or put the Gate Corporation in charge of it—which would accomplish the same thing."

"So how do you plan to win? I'm sure you could fight them off for a long time. But their population is, what, eight thousand times as big as all the colonies put together? There is no way they won't take back control eventually."

"Well, that's what we thought. That's why we've been keeping things quiet and not making our move. Some radicals around here were getting frustrated...coming up with some pretty terrifying plans...plans where a lot of people get hurt. They always get outvoted, but we've been afraid for a while they might splinter off from the movement and start acting on their own. But then that alien ship showed up."

"It's gone, and probably not coming back."

"It isn't gone. At least, it wasn't when we left."

"What do you mean?"

"I mean, we have someone at Orbital Control. As soon as that ship showed up he started feeding me telemetry. And the radio conversation. It's all here," he tapped the mini comp on his wrist, "and in the report that I sent to my superiors, with my comments, as soon as we stepped off the Gate. You see," he went on, "a stellar system is really huge. We forget how huge, because Gate travel is instantaneous. And that ship, even though it turned away from Earth, is going much slower than we know it can. Right now they are only just past the orbit of Mars. They're still refusing to answer messages from the Terrans. But I bet they would talk to you."

"I see," she said, trying to keep her voice flat, "so in other words, you already knew everything, and all of this was just so I could get you the ship."

"It's not like that! I would have brought you here anyway."

"It's fine, Brett. I'm willing to help. I was telling the truth about which side I'm on. I was being straight with you the whole time."

He began to say something, then stopped, apparently at a loss.

She sat silently, nursing the dregs of her sarsaparilla, and not looking at Brett.

"Here comes my boss," said Brett, as an older and stouter version of himself rounded the corner, wearing the same jeans and denim work shirt that seemed almost a uniform for the Jackpotters, "Commissioner," he began, "allow me to introduce Linda Harris of Morning Glory. Linda, this is Colonial Commissioner Andrew Fisher."

"Charmed to meet you, Young Lady," said the older Fisher, squeezing Linda's hand. "My son has been telling me quite a lot about you in his letters home."

"That's interesting. He never told me that he was the son of a commissioner. Or that he was a lieutenant, for that matter."

"Actually, I resigned that particular title last week. They just elected me consul, and I was already a militia general. Two government jobs at once were enough. But Brett only has one. He's my intelligence officer. You can probably see why he doesn't advertise that on Earth, though." The consul smiled, and she found she liked him a great deal, for most of the same reasons she had been attracted to his son. *Well, well, I guess I have a "type,"* she thought, *and they seem to breed them here on Jackpot.*

"Congratulations, Consul."

"Thanks. Now time is short. Our next scheduled translation to the belt is coming up in under two hours, and there isn't another until next week."

"Belt?" asked Linda.

"Sol's asteroid belt. The belters are technically on Terra's side, but they've been trading with us for a year—mostly fresh food in exchange for stuff that's easier to manufacture in zero-*g*—and they clearly hope we win independence because it will make their own bargaining position stronger.

"One of their major habitats is close enough to where the ship is that you should be able to connect with them long before Terra can get anyone out there. So we're going to send you through to them with a message saying that we'd really appreciate any help they can give. Worst they'll do is send you back Monday morning, but I think they'll help—they usually do.

"Anyway, that's the mission. The other thing I need to tell you relates to your own status. As far as we're concerned, Morning Glory belongs to you, and you speak for it the same way I and Sheila, that's the other consul, speak for Jackpot. All of the lost colonies need to stick together. If you decide to get some people together and go back, we'll consider you to be an independent ally. We'll even lend you tools and supplies and such, because that's what neighbors do. Even if you don't, the planet belongs to you now, not the Gate Corp or Terra. That's my official position, and I just wanted you to know."

"Thanks sir. I really appreciate all that."

"Now time is short, and I don't want to make you sit here talking to an old man. Do anything you want, but make sure you're on the Gate pad at 15:48. I might suggest popping into the dry goods store down the street and picking up some toiletries and a change of clothes. You'll be gone for a couple nights, and everything in the belt is overpriced. Brett can have them put it on our ranch's tab."

Slightly over two hours later Linda and Brett stood by a communications alcove in the asteroid habitat's cramped main operations center. "Cramped", seemed to describe every part of the habitat she had passed through so far. Nor did the belters seem to believe in windows. If it weren't for the low and slightly erratic gravity generated by the habitat's spin she could easily have imagined herself in an older, unusually claustrophobic, office building on Earth—not conditions calculated to make a girl from the prairie feel comfortable.

The communications tech was asking Brett a question about frequencies. He looked at Linda, who merely shrugged, "I couldn't see any numbers on the equipment, but they said it was one of the normal working frequencies."

"Normal frequency," grumbled a tech, "whatever that is. I'll try the near-Earth hailing frequency. After that it will just be guessing. I'll use my dish. The signal's still gonna spread, but at least it will miss Earth's orbitals." He began turning dials and speaking into his headset, "Alien Vessel, this is Habitat Bravo-Charlie. Alien Vessel, this is Habitat Bravo-Charlie..."

"Got 'em." He announced, after several tries, "Pretty strong signal too." He switched his mic back on, "Alien Vessel, roger your suggested adjustments. Please stand by for the Queen of Morning Glory."

"What did you just call me?" asked Linda, shocked and embarrassed.

"Don't look at me. I'm just paraphrasing what your boyfriend there told us. Anyway, pick up that headset before they get bored and hang up."

There was only one chair in the radio alcove and the tech was in it, so Linda leaned against the wall, close enough to the console that the headset cord would reach.

"Mom," she said, "it's Linda. Don't trust Earth. If you can make it here, we have a place in the asteroid belt where you can dock."

Chapter 10

ARRANGING THE RENDEZVOUS between the ship and the habitat was much more complicated than Linda expected. At first several different belters tried rattling off incomprehensible strings of velocities, bearings and coordinates to Linda, who tried to repeat them over the radio. Apparently, though, Amy didn't understand them any better. Even after a harassed looking mining pilot took the chair and talked to the ship directly things barely improved. Not only were Rah'ktll's controls calibrated in different units than the belters used (which anyone could have predicted, had they stopped to think about it), but the fundamental notation seemed different.

Finally, they found a way for the ship to home in on a laser. "Why didn't they just try that in the first place?" she asked a tech that seemed less busy than the others.

"Because none of our ships could follow a straight course like that." said the young woman, who looked surprised that Linda would ask what, to her, must seem an elementary question, "Uh, it's like...any time our ships go more than a short distance they move in a conic section so they can use gravity."

"Conic section?" asked Linda, "You mean like a parabola?"

"Yeah, or more often an ellipse, because that's what a natural orbit looks like. You are traveling along one curve, then you add or subtract v at the right time to move onto a different curve. If you try to just go any old direction and ignore gravity and inertia, then you burn through your fuel in no time. But they don't seem to care. They drive that ship like a car—that's the word for one of those ground vehicles, right? They just point it where they want it to go and use as much energy as they need, like they aren't worried about ever running out and whatever kind of orbit they end up in is fine." She rolled her eyes, "It's just not natural."

"Then why do you even have a laser?"

The tech looked like she had already suspected Linda was retarded, and was now sure of it. "For communications," she said, "Do you think we usually yell our business out on FM radio for everyone in the system to hear?"

"Okay, that makes sense. Thanks for explaining." Linda knew her own upbringing had been unusual by Terran standards, but she suspected that belters had a different education entirely. She wondered if they studied orbital mechanics and communication lasers before or after their ABCs.

Once the belters turned on their laser Aorhs had no trouble following it in. The ship's normal space piloting interface was mostly automated; once you told it where you wanted to go it was good at smoothly doing what it needed to do to get you there. Amy didn't know if the trouble communicating earlier had been because of her own self-taught and bilingual astrogation skills, or because the Terran system was actually that different. That was probably the least important of the things she currently didn't understand. "I wish we knew we could trust these belt-rats," she said to Aorhs, who occupied the other control station, "I'm still not sure which side they're on, or even what the sides are."

"If you don't know the difference between groups of humans, then how can a poor alien? Was that not your daughter on the com?"

"It sounded like the same person we talked to before, whom I want to believe was really Linda and not some sort of weird mind game. But given that I don't know which side she's on, nor whether she hates me, that isn't very helpful. Also, she refused to explain how she got out here ahead of us. The only way she could have done that is with the Gate. If she's on the side that controls the Gate, does that mean that the military is on the other side?"

"Again, you are the human. This one just drives the ship. Do you wish to break off and retreat until we know more?"

"No. If there is any chance that that is Linda over there, then I need to see her. I just wish we knew what we were walking into. When we get there we aren't going to try a hard dock, even if they tell us to, which they shouldn't, because the systems aren't compatible. I'm going to go over alone and keep my com up. If you hear me say the word 'accordion' or if I go more than eighteen merchaks without contacting you, blast the hell out of that station with everything you have." Although unarmed by the standards of the race that built her, the vessel possessed certain systems that could project massive levels of EM energy. A few seconds of that should fry half the systems on a civilian space station, possibly giving Amy a chance to escape in the resulting confusion, "Then wait five *merchaks* to see if I get out," she continued, "If not, give up on me and get out of this system."

"Traveling the stars alone has no appeal to this one. Besides, you are the astrogator."

"Hopefully it won't come to that. But it's clear that both groups of humans want this ship pretty badly, and I don't think we should hand it over unless we know why."

Once the ship had synced itself to the motion of the asteroid station, aligning itself with one pole the nonrotating core section, Amy left Aohrs on the bridge and went down to the lock to suit up. Remembering her experience on the last occasion she had spacewalked to a station, she clipped an extra patch kit to the belt of her suit. The belters had offered to extend a soft-sided docking tube with handlines to facilitate her trip, but she had refused. As she had pointed out to Aorhs, the process of rigging the tube would have provided excellent cover to sneak an EVA team into the ship's blind spots. She wondered if she had been this paranoid when she was still human.

This time she glided across the void in good form and without mishap. As she caught one of the grab rails and smoothly swung to a stop inside the station's airlock she wondered if any of the belters had been watching. She thought about how, for a dirt-side biologist, she was catching on pretty well to spacefaring. Then she told herself to focus; this was a bad time to get distracted. She dogged the outer hatch and waited for the lights on the opposite door to go green, indicating that the pressure had equalized. Then, feet hooked on the handrail in case she needed to launch herself in some direction, she undogged the inner door and shoved it aside.

Three people floated in the corridor on the other side of the door, two men and a woman. One man, obviously completely comfortable in microgravity, was in early middle age. He had a buzz haircut and wore the coveralls that had been space station work dress since the dawn of astronautics—obviously a belter, in other words. The other man looked around twenty. He was solidly built with a pleasantly masculine face. Like the woman he was dressed, incongruously, in jeans and a cotton work shirt and gripped a nearby handhold, clearly uncomfortable in zero-*g*. Amy's eyes slid over the two men and dismissed them completely. Her full attention was on the young woman, the woman who had her face and eyes, and Jim's rangy build. "Linda?" she asked. Then, remembering that she was wearing a spacesuit, she found the toggle that turned on the external speaker. "Linda? Is that you?"

"Hello Mom. It's been a long time, huh?"

Amy began to launch herself at Linda to hug her, then stopped almost immediately (luckily, she still had a toe under the rail), realizing her action might be misinterpreted. The younger man's right hand shot to his hip, where she suspected a pistol usually lived, apparently without his volition, and risked starting him spinning.

"Sorry," said Amy. She unlatched her helmet and took it off so they could have a better view of her face. She unclipped the headset from inside and hung the hook of it over her ear, then clipped the helmet to one of the carabiners on her belt, "I'm really not dangerous. I'm just excited to see other humans after all these years. Especially you, Linda."

"Are you?" asked Linda, "a human, I mean?"

"Yes and no. You already know I've been infected with what I've come to believe is a deliberately engineered biological agent. It has made some structural and metabolic changes to my body, but I still look, and more importantly think, like any other human. You don't need to worry about catching it; it can only be transferred by the secretions of a special secondary salivary gland. Sorry, that sounds a bit clinical, but I am a biologist."

"Why would anyone ever want to engineer an agent like that?" asked the younger man.

"Honestly, we aren't sure. I caught it from my friend, who caught it from a third race, and that race might not have even been the ones who created it. All we know about them is that they were aliens, and probably didn't think like us at all. Maybe it was an attempt to modify colonists for a special environment. Maybe it was an April Fool's joke that got out of hand. I don't think we'll ever know."

"So are you saying the virus isn't even from Morning Glory?" asked Linda.

"Absolutely not. Aorhs' crew caught it when they visited another ship in deep space, before they ever came to Morning Glory."

"Crew?" asked the belter, "how big a crew do you have there?" He looked over her shoulder at the airlock door as if he expected an alien horde to stream through it at any moment.

"Just me and Aorhs. The rest of his crew died a long time ago. He was in cold sleep until after we had already settled in on Morning Glory, waiting for a rescue from his own planet. He thinks that his computer woke him up when it started detecting signals from our colony.

"My turn to ask some questions," said Amy, "what the hell has happened on Earth over the last fifteen years? Who's fighting whom and which side are you guys on? Also, why did the Gate stop working, what happened on Morning Glory after I left, and how did you get out here ahead of me? I'll probably think of more, but those will do for a start."

The other three looked at each other for a moment. Finally, the younger man said, "It's going to take a while to explain. Do you want to take your suit off and come in for a while? Wait, before we do that, this is Station Commander Phelps. I'm Lieutenant Brett Fisher, 1st Jackpot Militia." He moved towards her painstakingly, using the grips on the wall. Once he was close enough, he held out a hand for her to shake. She took it in the gauntlet of her suit, remembering only belatedly that the outsides of spacesuits tend to be extremely cold. He didn't flinch, though, either because the suit was already warming, or because he was simply not the kind of man who flinched.

"Thank you, Brett," she said, "in that case I think I will come in."

Once Amy understood the situation, she agreed to help the colonies, provided Aorhs would remain in command of the ship. Linda couldn't tell whether she had decided this from any genuine ideological enthusiasm, or simply because that was the side Linda had chosen. Aorhs, for his part, seemed happy enough to follow wherever Amy went. Difficulties became apparent, however, when the colonial leadership, speaking through Brett, asked her to take the ship to Jackpot and she admitted that she had no idea how to get there. "I'm sure we can find it eventually," she told him, "if you know what the stars look like from there. But keep in mind it took us fifteen years to find Earth. Before we go, though, we need someone who understands ships to give the Rah'ktll a real going-over. She's an old ship, and we've been running her continuously since we left Morning Glory. We've already had some equipment failures."

"That's a problem. We don't know if the Terrans know we're here, but they will figure it out soon. Not only was the ship running in this direction the last time they saw her, but this is still nominally a Terran station. They gate gear and people back and forth all the time. Any day now some loyalist is going to come aboard, notice that there's a ship parked here, and get a message back. It would have happened by now, if belters put more windows on their stations."

They eventually compromised. The engineers from the habitat would do their best to give the ship a safety inspection before she left. While no one understood the ship's more esoteric systems, they would probably be able to spot problems like metal fatigue, cracked hoses, and loose fasteners. They did. The ship stayed in place for more and more days while technicians EVAed back and forth, fixing the problems they knew how to identify, and hoping that none of the ones they couldn't find would prove fatal.

Aorhs, with help from Amy and, surprisingly, Brett (who had majored in engineering during his aborted stint in college), serviced the systems, especially the cold sleep chambers, which had been under his purview as ship's surgeon.

The plan called for Amy and Aorhs, along with a crew of volunteer technicians from Jackpot and the belt, to take the ship to the abandoned Thule-B station, for which Amy had coordinates. This was somewhat risky, since the Terrans might decide to reoccupy the station, but the opportunity to use the station's equipment and stores seemed to outweigh the danger. The only other colony system whose location Amy knew was Morning Glory, which had no resources at all. They briefly considered moving to another of the belt habitats, but no one was sure which station commanders could be trusted with such an important secret.

The ship would carry tools, raw materials, and reference books. As soon as they woke from cold sleep the new crew would work watch on watch to understand how the technology worked and to fix any remaining wear and damage. Brett had volunteered for this team, but been afraid that he wouldn't be allowed to go until orders actually arrived, telling him that his commission had been transferred and that he was now a lieutenant (senior grade) in the newly created Colonial Space Force, assigned as third officer of the Rah'ktll.

Meanwhile another part of the crew, led by Amy (commander, CSF) would try to finally crack the problem of converting real-space stellar coordinates into a form that the Merspis' astrogation system would accept. For this she would be assisted by a mining tug pilot from the belt. The problem had still seemed hopeless until someone remembered a young woman on New Dream who was said to be a math and physics prodigy, and who had just, at the age of fifteen, been offered a scholarship to MIT. She was visited by separatist leaders who reminded her of her patriotic duty and offered to reimburse the value of the scholarship from colonial coffers as soon as the troubles were over. What had finally convinced her to go though, as she later explained to Brett, was the chance to serve on the first true starship that humanity had ever encountered. She arrived through the Gate wide-eyed and distracted, then immediately removed to the astrogator's nook on the Rah'ktll, where she stayed twenty-four hours a day from then on, learning to commune with the alien computers.

For Linda, it was an exciting time. With all the people passing though, not to mention all the work (it turned out that, even amid the advanced technology of two different races, people could still find plenty of unskilled scut work for someone like her to do), she didn't even notice the cramped conditions of the habitat, in which they were now forced to "hot bunk" with the shift opposite theirs. Her relations with both her mother and Brett were polite, but tense, because she didn't really trust either of them—one because she was still a space monster, and the other one because he had misled her to use her for his movement... which wasn't fair of her, she kept telling herself. After all, it was her movement too, and he hadn't really kept that much from her. And it wasn't like they had been dating, or anything. They had never even kissed. But it had felt so romantic, when he had asked her to run away to Jackpot with him...and then it had turned out to not be romantic at all.

Amy asked Linda to join them on the ship. Linda politely declined. She had none of the skills which were needed on that mission. She would go to Jackpot for the duration. The skills she did have—hunting, cooking, gardening, and survival—should actually be useful on a ranching world. More importantly, there was talk of a Colonial Congress, and it still seemed that, under the influence of General Fisher, they were going to let her represent Morning Glory (population: one human and two monsters, none of them currently in residence). That would be far more useful and meaningful than being a passenger on the ship, cooped up with two people in whose presence she currently felt so awkward.

Finally, everything was ready. Both crews—that of the ship and that of the station—gathered in the station's dining area for a send-off party. A hearty barbecue dinner had been cooked on Jackpot and gated over for the occasion. Brett had just made a toast and raised his sarsaparilla when the lights went red and every alarm in the station began going off at once.

Chapter 11

EVERYONE BEGAN SHOUTING over each other and running in different directions based on what they thought was happening. It looked like the whole station would dissolve into panic and confusion when a gunshot—an actual gunshot, rang out. Everyone stopped dead, then turned to stare at Brett. He had drawn the big handgun that he had begun wearing again and fired into a tray of meat on the table in front of him, not wanting to puncture any bulkheads.

"Ladies and gentlemen," he announced, "all that noise means that we've just had an unscheduled Gate transition. We haven't blown up yet, so it isn't a bomb. Therefore, I assume we now have Terran Marines on this station. Captain Aorhs, I respectfully suggest you lead as many of the crew as possible to the ship. With your permission I would like to lead a small party to try to delay the intruders."

Aorhs dipped his chin. "Very well."

"Commander Phelps," Brett went on, "we are very grateful for all the help you and your people have given us and we're sorry we brought this on you. I suggest all of you lock yourselves in your quarters until things settle down. You can tell them we held guns on you and made you work for us."

Phelps bared his teeth, "Anyone who wants to do that is free to and I won't hold it against them. As for me, I'm going to get to Ops and see if I can give you any help."

Brett nodded. "Thanks Sir. Now, besides me, who's armed?"

Five people, all Jackpotters, raised their hands.

"Hwang, you're our best welder. Schmitt, you're our only software engineer. Give your guns to someone else and go to the ship," said Brett. "Now. That's an order."

Linda pushed her way in front of Johann Schmitt and held out her hand for his weapon. "Come on," she said, "we're in a hurry."

Brett saw. "Linda? Not you..." for the first time she heard doubt in his voice.

"Brett, I know as much about fighting as anyone here and I'm the only one you definitely don't need on the ship, because I'm not part of the crew."

"Do it," he told Schmitt, not looking at all happy. Schmitt passed Linda a leather gun belt that held an automatic, an extra clip, and a good-size folding knife. The smallest hole still left it far too big for her hips, so she hung it across her shoulders like a bandolier. She took the gun out and inspected it under the red emergency lights, jacking a round into the chamber and making sure she could find the safety and the clip release. It wasn't Mary's old arbalest, but it would do.

"Okay," said Brett, "remember that our job is to slow them down, not to fight to the end. Use any cover you find. They wear body armor, so shoot for the knees or face. And most importantly, watch where you're shooting. If you puncture an outside wall everyone dies. Anyone not understand that? Okay, Linda, Jose, we're going spinward. Everyone else go counter-spin." The Gate pad was nearly all the way around the rotating central ring of the station from where they were now. Apparently, Brett was trying to trap the intruders between the two halves of his impromptu squad. The airlock to the ship, being in the central shaft, was a shorter trip. But, Linda remembered, they didn't have enough suits for the crew to go over at once. Someone would have to bring suits back across for the second wave to use.

As they passed down the corridor Brett pulled two wireless headsets from a cabinet under a com panel and tossed them to Jose and herself. For the first time she realized that he had been wearing an earbud the whole time, which likely contained a built-in mic. He had probably been wearing it constantly over the past few days. "Channel One," he told them.

They rounded a corner and gunfire lashed out at them. Linda threw herself backwards, using the corner as cover. Jose moved too slowly and went down. From where she was she could see that he was missing the top half of his head. She dropped to her knees and risked a quick peak around the corner, pulling back as bullets zinged through the space where her head had been. She had seen that Brett was still on his feet, body plastered into an alcove that should have been too small for him. Suddenly, all the lights went out.

"Quick Brett, get back!" she heard from her earphones, and realized it was the station commander's voice from Ops. "Thanks!" she heard Brett say, shortly after she heard his bulk hit the deck on her leg of the el in the corridor.

"Brett and Linda, there are four in the corridor ahead of you. One's down but I don't know if he's out. I shut bulkheads around them and dumped Halon on them. They have some kind of air masks but that one was too slow putting his on. There are two other four-person teams. Move back fifteen yards and you'll find a ladder. Take it up and you might be able to get around them." Linda knelt and felt for Jose's gun. Finding it she jammed it into the waistband of her jeans then groped her way back along the dark corridor, Brett next to her.

"Anyone from our other team on the com yet?" asked Brett, and waited for an answer.

"I don't think they know to pick up headsets," said Phelps. "By the way, the other side only have pistols, not rifles. They're probably afraid of holing the bulkheads, same as us."

Linda found the ladder shoved Brett towards it. "Go, I'm right behind."

"Damn," said Phelp's voice. "They just jimmied the door. They're coming behind you."

Brett squatted by the ladder, pointing his gun down into the corridor they had just left. Linda did the same. Red flashlights illuminated the corridor below, coming their way. As soon as the lights were directly below Linda worked her finger rapidly, spraying the corridor with bullets, then rolled backwards, Brett doing the same next to her. She got to her scrambled to her feet and ran down the corridor. She was quite sure she had seen Sergeant Li's face in the corridor, by the light of her own muzzle flash. She didn't know if she hoped that she had hit him, or was afraid she had. Why did it have to be them? But she had always known that the special platoon would be the first through the Gate. In the dark she ran straight into a wall, which knocked the breath out of her and caused her to drop her gun.

A flash lit the corridor behind her where a Marine had thrown a grenade up the ladder. Shrapnel whizzed down the hallway around her. Luckily, she was still facing the wall so none of it hit her face. As it was, she was cut in several places, but none felt deep or serious. As if she could tell, in the dark with all hell breaking loose on the station.

Suddenly the red lights came back on, Phelps having realized that the darkness was now hindering his own side at least as much as the Marines. They were in a tee intersection. Brett took cover behind a wall and shot a few rounds across the ladder hole, then broke left down the corridor to another alcove. Pulling out Jose's gun, Lisa shot a couple rounds of her own, then leapfrogged Brett, pulling behind the wall of a side corridor. They waited for the Marines to come down the corridor into their fire.

"Linda, behind you!" said Phelps, too late. Linda was suddenly slammed against the wall behind which she had been hiding, then falling. Only once she was on the floor did she feel the pain in her shoulder. She had no idea where her gun had gone. With one working arm she tried to push herself towards some sort of cover, only to find herself rolled over and the muzzle of a pistol pointed directly at her nose.

"Please stay still, Linda," said Andrea Hardy, "I really, really don't want to have to shoot you again."

Linda passed out at that point, which was as sensible a move as any.

When she woke up, she was laying on her back. Moving even slightly caused such incredible pain in her right shoulder that she decided to stay immobile forever. She heard voices: Andrea asking someone about a "butcher's bill." That didn't make sense. Was she talking about the barbecue? She heard Sergeant Li's voice, and was glad she hadn't killed him after all, "Four dead. Three of theirs, one of ours. Nearly everyone on both sides are injured, but mostly superficial. Linda Harris is the only really bad one. That shoulder's completely trashed, and she caught a fair amount of shrapnel. I think one of her kidneys is sliced, maybe intestines. I think we should gate her out in the very first load."

That doesn't sound good, thought Linda, and passed out again.

The next time she woke, she heard Brett and someone else, she thought it was Li again, arguing. The words they were saying didn't make much sense, though. The phrase "unlawful combatant" came up more than once, Brett kept repeating his name and rank and a series of numbers, and there was something about uniforms. Linda decided she was dreaming it, and slipped away again.

The third and final time she woke up she had been propped up on her side, bad shoulder up. She opened her eyes, but it was too bright and she closed them again.

"Hey kid, are you still with us?" asked Andrea.

"Andrea? Are you the one who shot me?"

"Unfortunately, yes. I want you to know it was nothing personal, just work. No hard feelings?"

"'S alright. Someone else would have, if you hadn't"

"Probably." Silence, for a minute or so.

"Okay, I lied," said Andrea, "it was a little personal. I'm still kind of pissed at you for the way you left. I think I understand why you did what you did, but you could at least have said goodbye first."

"I'm sorry. I'm really sorry. I'm sorry I ran out on you and I'm sorry I shot at Sergeant Li, and I'm sorry for this whole mess, which I think is kinda my fault. I wish you'd never come and gotten me off Morning Glory."

"Hey, an apology is well and good, but that's a bit much, don't you think? After all, I did shoot you. I figure that makes us square. Friends?"

"Friends."

"By the way, you tagged Li pretty good. One through the meaty part of his arm and two in the chest. He'll have some bruises under his armor in the morning. Being Li, though, he's not mad at all. If anything, he seems proud of you."

"Tell him I'm sorry, anyway."

"I will. Listen, I'm glad we got to talk. Our first Gate transition is coming up, and I'm sending you on it. You'll probably be in hospital for a while, and I may not be allowed to visit you."

"Okay. We're in kind of a lot of trouble, aren't we?"

"Honestly, yes. You took over a station in a way that looks a lot like piracy, although stories from the station crew seem to vary widely. You fired on Terran Marines and killed one of us. Plus none of the colonies has actually seceded yet and we wouldn't recognize them if they did, which makes you domestic terrorists, or at least criminals. When you get better you are going to want to hire the best civilian lawyer you can find."

"That's what I figured." Marines leaned over her and rolled her onto a stretcher.

"One last question," she asked, as they hoisted her up, "did the ship get away?"

"Yes," replied Andrea, "they..."

Suddenly the room was filled with gunfire and motion. The stretcher dropped, sending Linda to the floor again in a blast of pain that almost made her black out again. She opened her eyes and somehow managed to roll up on her side again. Directly ahead of her, she saw Aorhs and Andrea rolling across the floor, grappling frantically. Andrea had her combat knife out and was driving it repeatedly into his side while she tried to fend off his fangs with her other hand. Ignoring the knife he caught hold of the warding off-hand and twisted it until it snapped.

"Aorhs, don't kill her!" Linda yelled as he drew back his head to tear out the lieutenant's throat. He must have heard her, because he paused for an instant. Suddenly Li hove into Lina's view, pistol in the hand that wasn't in a sling. From short range he shot Aorhs in the head, then shot him again as he fell away from Lieutenant Hardy. Li bent to help his officer, but Amy crashed into him, bearing the big man down under her with sheer velocity and ferocity. She got up, but he didn't. Her fangs, still out, were stained with blood and gore coated the front of her coverall.

Amy stooped and picked up Andrea Hardy by the throat, twisting the knife effortlessly out of her hand. She stood, slowly strangling the lieutenant, who batted at her ineffectually with her good arm.

"No Mom, don't kill her! Please!" Linda yelled for the second time. Amy looked down at Linda, and the sight of her daughter seemed to calm her. She dropped Hardy to the ground with an unpleasant crunching noise and retracted her fangs, giving her face a much more humanoid appearance. "Why shouldn't I kill her? Isn't this war? They already killed our crewmates and shot you."

"Because she's my friend. She's the enemy, but she's still my friend."

Amy looked like she was trying to parse this paradoxical statement then gave up and just said, "I'm sorry Linda. I'm so sorry this happened to you! I should have stayed here on the station with you and protected you."

"Don't worry about it, Mom. You just saved me from a firing squad, or at least prison, so let's call it even."

"Don't just stand there talking," said Brett's voice, "Linda's hurt really bad. You need to get her to the Gate pad before it transitions, so they can take her to a hospital on Earth."

"Brett, I did mention the probable firing squad, didn't I?" said Linda.

"Doesn't matter anyway," said Phelps, "their Gate just transited. Who knows when, or if, they'll schedule another. Here, Brett, roll over and I'll untie you. Doesn't Jackpot have hospitals?"

"One, but it's basic. Anyway, I don't even remember when our own next transit is. Sometime tomorrow, I think?"

"Those bastards just killed the only medic I know," said Amy. She stood over Aorhs' body, tears streaming down her face. Apparently even the virus couldn't heal a bullet to the head.

"They've almost killed your daughter Amy!" said Brett. "We've got to do something right now. Look, she's bleeding through her dressings."

"I'll last a few more minutes," said Linda, without knowing whether that was true, "Andrea—Lieutenant Hardy, that is—isn't moving. Someone check her."

Phelps knelt over Andrea. "She's got a pulse, but it's pretty weak. Dent in the back of her head, so definitely concussed, and that arm is compound fractured."

"You guys have got to help her, and any other Marines, if they're still alive," said Linda, "they patched me up after I was hurt," she remembered something that she hadn't thought about recently, "that's an order. I'm the head of state of a planet, so I outrank all of you."

"What's she talking about?" asked Amy, "is she delirious?"

"Actually," said Brett, "she might technically be right. But regardless, Linda, we will happily help everyone but, as already mentioned, our medic is dead and we can't get to a hospital until some time tomorrow."

"Know what, you jerk, you have a terrible bedside manner!" she told him, and started laughing. She immediately stopped, because moving hurt too badly.

"Linda," said Amy, "there is a way to heal both of you, but I won't force it on you, and I'll let you decide for her, since she's unconscious, and you're her friend."

"You mean the virus. You're offering to turn me into the same sort of monster that haunted my entire childhood."

"Like I said, I'll respect your decision. But am I such a monster? Was Aorhs a monster?"

"You realize you just tore the throat out of one of my other friends?"

"Let her help you, Linda," put in Brett, "Are fangs really so different from a gun, or a knife? Amy's a soldier now, just like me, and just like you were today. You and I were shooting at these same people a few hours ago." he moved around and knelt by her face. "The fact is, you're important. You're the Survivor of Morning Glory, which makes you a symbol for all the lost colonies. You are a congressional delegate. You're a hero of the first battle of the war. If you live you're going to be a leader in the colonies for a long time. And yeah, if you want to go back to Morning Glory and be a queen none of us is going to stop you and a lot of us might go with you.

"But all that isn't why you're important, or isn't the only reason." He reached down, found her good hand, and squeezed it. "The thing is, you're really important to me. I realized just how important when we were fighting, and when I saw you shot. I don't think I could take it if you died. Please, Linda, let your mother help you."

"Okay," said Linda, "I think that most of that is a load of crap. But I guess I need to live so I can find out. So, okay, Mom, monster me up. But do Andrea first. She's probably going to shoot me again when she finds out I told you to, but I can't just let her die, either."

Linda floated weightless in the station core. Her stomach was distended from all the meat she had eaten earlier. Between the two of them she and Andrea had finished the leftover meat from the barbecue party, then made a good start on a hastily thawed side of beef from the ship.

"Feeling better now?" asked Brett.

"Sure," she said, "now we're just ravenous, instead of insane."

He smiled, "Good thing you two are headed to a planet that specializes in meat." Andrea, technically a prisoner of war, had given her parole and would accompany Linda back to Jackpot. She had turned out to be surprisingly philosophical about the situation, once she was lucid and had heard the story. She had even asked Brett if he had any single brothers back home. He did, apparently, but they were both younger.

Amy and Brett, the officers, were the last to board the Rah'ktll. "It's time to go," said Amy, "they need to get to the Gate and then we need to wreck this station."

The Jackpot Gate had been running at half hour intervals, evacuating the station crew, carrying their personal effects and every useful piece of technology that they could unbolt. Commander Phelps and a pair of techs would be the last ones through. Before they left they would shut down and eject the main reactor. Then, as its last act before going into hyperspace, the Rah'ktll would spray the station with EM radiation, slagging any remaining electronics. Anyone who decided to gate there in the future would find a station with no power and all of its equipment either stripped or destroyed.

"I'll see you on Jackpot," said Amy, "as fast as we can possibly make it."

"We'll both see you," said Brett. He swallowed and clenched his fists, as if wracked by indecision. Then, to her great surprise, he launched himself by kicking off a nearby console, collided with her, and began kissing her with little skill, but great gusto. Since neither of them was proficient in zero-*g* yet, they immediately pinwheeled out of control like a drunken octopus. Linda didn't mind, even when they slammed into the opposite wall in a tangle of arms and legs. Finally, when things had begun to slow down a bit, she broke the lip-lock and shoved him towards the airlock. "You better come back, after that!" she said. He just grinned and blew a kiss before clawing his way awkwardly through the hatch.

"Well, it was about time that happened," said Andrea, and they made their way towards the Gate. Linda felt heat rise to her face. "Brave man, though," Andrea continued, "to stick his tongue in there with the fangs."